The Virtual Vandal

Read all the books in the
**TOM SWIFT INVENTORS'
ACADEMY** series!

The Drone Pursuit
The Sonic Breach
Restricted Access
The Virtual Vandal

TOM SWIFT
INVENTORS' ACADEMY

– BOOK 4 –

The Virtual Vandal

VICTOR APPLETON

Aladdin

NEW YORK LONDON TORONTO SYDNEY NEW DELHI

ALADDIN

An imprint of Simon & Schuster Children's Publishing Division
1230 Avenue of the Americas, New York, New York 10020
First Aladdin hardcover edition March 2020
Text copyright © 2020 by Simon & Schuster, Inc.
Jacket illustration copyright © 2020 by Kevin Keele
TOM SWIFT, TOM SWIFT INVENTORS' ACADEMY, and related logos are trademarks of Simon & Schuster, Inc.
Also available in an Aladdin paperback edition.
All rights reserved, including the right of reproduction in whole or in part in any form.
ALADDIN and related logo are registered trademarks of Simon & Schuster, Inc.
For information about special discounts for bulk purchases, please contact Simon & Schuster Special Sales at 1-866-506-1949 or business@simonandschuster.com.
The Simon & Schuster Speakers Bureau can bring authors to your live event.
For more information or to book an event contact the Simon & Schuster Speakers Bureau at 1-866-248-3049 or visit our website at www.simonspeakers.com.
Jacket designed by Heather Palisi
Interior designed by Mike Rosamilia
The text of this book was set in Adobe Caslon Pro.
Manufactured in the United States of America 0220 FFG
10 9 8 7 6 5 4 3 2 1
Library of Congress Cataloging-in-Publication Data
Names: Appleton, Victor, author.
Title: The virtual vandal / by Victor Appleton.
Description: First Aladdin hardcover/paperback edition. | New York : Aladdin, 2020. |
Series: Tom Swift Inventors' Academy | Summary: Someone is sabotaging student projects, and all signs point to Tom's friend Sam as the culprit, so Tom and his friends set out to clear her name.
Identifiers: LCCN 2019015056 (print) | LCCN 2019018137 (eBook) |
ISBN 9781534436411 (eBook) | ISBN 9781534436398 (pbk) | ISBN 9781534436404 (hc)
Subjects: | CYAC: Inventors—Fiction. | Vandalism—Fiction. | Virtual reality—Fiction. |
Schools—Fiction. | Friendship—Fiction. | Science fiction.
Classification: LCC PZ7.A652 (eBook) | LCC PZ7.A652 Vir 2020 (print) |
DDC [Fic]—dc23
LC record available at https://lccn.loc.gov/2019015056

Contents

Contents

The Simulation Demonstration

THE THREE OF US SLOWLY MADE OUR WAY UP THE dark steps. I led the way, followed by my friends Amy Hsu and Samantha Watson. As we stepped out onto the third floor, I aimed my flashlight into the empty corridor. I could feel my heart beating faster with anticipation.

"This is really creepy," Amy whispered. "Cool, but creepy."

"Why are you whispering?" Sam asked. "We're the only ones here."

"Because we're creeping around the school at night,"

Amy replied. "Even if it's not really . . ." She trailed off as she whipped her flashlight back down the stairs. Sam and I froze, listening.

Then Amy relaxed, and we continued down the hall. "Besides—" She went back to a whisper. "Noah might be spying on us."

"Of course he's spying on us," I said with a chuckle. "He worked too hard on this *not* to spy on us." I glanced around. "Isn't that right, dude?"

There was no reply.

"That would've been too easy, Swift," Sam said as she led the way down the dark corridor.

Noah Newton, my best friend, had created a special scavenger hunt for us. And the setting for this hunt? Our school, the Swift Academy of Science and Technology. At night, of course.

If the name of our school sounds familiar, it's because it was named after my father, Tom Swift Sr. He founded the academy with profits from his company, Swift Enterprises. If you think it would be cool to have all these places with your last name on them, you'd be wrong. Honestly, it just means I have to work harder to be a regular student like everyone else.

A flash of light burst through a nearby window. Soon after, the walls seemed to rattle with the deep boom of thunder.

"The thunderstorm is a nice touch," I said to Noah, wherever he was. He still didn't reply.

Sam stopped moving forward. "What was the clue again?"

Amy responded automatically. Having a photographic memory, she had already memorized it when she had first read it. "'Once on the third floor, don't be afraid of the dark,'" she replied. "'Find not the king of the jungle, but the king of the park.'"

"Who's the king of the park?" I asked.

"A lion is supposed to be the king of the jungle," Sam replied. "Even though they technically don't live in jungles."

"What about in Mrs. Livingston's classroom?" asked Amy. "She has a lion poster in there."

"It's worth a shot," I said.

We glided down the hallway toward our biology classroom. I swung open the door and reached for the light switch. I heard the switch click but the overhead lights didn't come on. The only light came through the windows and barely illuminated the room.

The three of us poured in and made our way to the wall behind Mrs. Livingston's desk. Hung there was a motivational poster about courage, sporting a large lion with a thick, shaggy mane. I'm not sure if Mrs. Livingston had it up there to remind us to be courageous and ask questions, or because of her notoriously difficult exams.

"Wait a minute," said Sam. She stopped moving. "The clue said *not* the king of the jungle."

"That's right," I agreed, glancing around. "But who would be king of the park?"

Amy pointed to a poster on the other side of the classroom. "What about that one?"

I turned and squinted across the room. I had completely forgotten that Mrs. Livingston also had a tyrannosaurus rex poster at the back of the classroom. It wasn't a motivational poster or anything; it was just part of a cool dinosaur display she had created. The exhibition also included a fossilized megalodon tooth, the fossilized femur of an Edmontosaurus, and a cast Mrs. Livingston made of a real dinosaur footprint (a small theropod of some kind).

"King of the park," Sam said, excitement rising in her voice. "Like Jurassic Park."

"Even though the T. rex really lived during the Cretaceous period," Amy added.

"Yeah, but *Cretaceous Park* doesn't have the same ring to it," I said as I made my way toward the poster.

We all gathered around it. On it, a huge T. rex stood in the clearing of a prehistoric forest. It grinned at us, its mouth full of jagged teeth.

"The poster is exactly the same," Amy observed. "Noah didn't add anything to it."

"Maybe he hid something behind it," Sam suggested. She reached out and grabbed the bottom left corner of the poster. But when she lifted up the flap, the corner jerked itself away from her and snapped back to the wall.

"What the . . . ," Sam began.

Then the entire poster began to expand. We stood back as the bottom of the picture slid down the wall and onto the baseboards. The top of the poster stretched up toward the ceiling as the entire thing grew. Soon, the image of the terrifying dinosaur covered the whole wall.

"What's going on?" asked Amy.

The dinosaur was now life-size. My heart raced as it glared down at us. Then, as if it couldn't get any stranger than that, the T. rex moved. Just a blink of an eye at first, and then one of its two-clawed hands closed.

"Did you just see that?!" Sam asked in an entire octave above her normal speaking voice.

Before anyone could answer, one of the dinosaur's huge feet stepped *out* of the poster. It scattered the fossil display and crashed down on a nearby desk. We moved back as the desk shattered.

Above us, the T. rex *leaned out* of the poster! Its long snout stretched and contorted as 2-D slowly became 3-D. As it loomed over us, it cocked its head and examined us with one large eye. Its mouth opened wider, long tendrils of saliva dripping down from above.

"Run!" I shouted.

The three of us bolted toward the door as the T. rex roared. I chanced a glance back to see the full-size tyrannosaurus rex on our tails, crashing through desks as it chased after us.

My heart raced faster as we ran out of the classroom and headed toward the closest stairwell. Amy and Sam shot past me as I checked behind us. There was no way that huge dinosaur would fit through the classroom door. . . .

Boy, was I wrong. The T. rex burst through the wall. Shattered cinderblocks and splintered wood ricocheted down the empty corridor as the creature skidded to a stop in the middle of the hallway. It sniffed and whipped its head in our direction. My blood turned to ice.

I flew down the stairs and caught up to my friends as they entered the first floor. I could hear the dinosaur barreling down the stairwell behind us. There probably wouldn't be any steps left by the time it reached the bottom.

"Unbelievable," Sam said as she glanced back.

We darted down the main corridor, toward the gym.

"What's that?" Amy asked, pointing ahead.

There was a small wooden box on the floor ahead of us. It sat conspicuously in the middle of the hallway, right in front of the open gym doors. We came to a stop next to it and I lifted the lid. Several long red cylinders lined the box.

"Is that dynamite?" Amy asked.

"We're supposed to stop a dinosaur with dynamite?" asked Sam.

As if on cue, the huge T. rex crashed to the bottom of the stairwell. Dust and debris filled the air as the dinosaur lumbered through the entryway and stomped into the first-floor hallway. It paused to give another bone-chilling roar before moving in our direction.

I pulled out one of the sticks of dynamite and turned it over in my hands.

"It doesn't have a fuse," I said disarmingly.

"Does anyone have matches or a lighter?" asked Sam. "How could we light it even if it did have a fuse?"

The T. rex roared again as it ran closer.

"W-w—what do we do?" stammered Amy.

"Oh man," said a familiar voice. "You guys are *so* going to get eaten."

Suddenly, as if by magic, Noah appeared between us and the charging dinosaur. He reached into the wooden box and pulled out a stick of dynamite. Noah removed a clear cap off one end of the stick and brought it toward the other end, and then I realized that it wasn't dynamite at all. With a quick motion, he scraped them against each other, like striking a match. The road flare ignited with a hissing, sparking red light.

"Check it out," Noah said as he turned to face the charging beast.

The T. rex slid to a stop in front of the flare. Its giant

head stretched forward and tracked the bright light as Noah moved it from right to left, and then left to right. Then Noah tossed the flare through the open gym doors. The dinosaur took off after it, twisting the metal doorjamb as it squeezed through the entryway. We watched as it disappeared into the dark gym.

"Aw, man," Sam said. "We should've guessed that one."

"I put a hint in the clue and everything," Noah said.

"The same way Dr. Grant tried to distract the T. rex in *Jurassic Park*," Amy added.

"Except it worked when I did it," said Noah.

"Dude," I said, turning to my best friend. "That was awesome!" I extended a fist toward him.

Noah reached out and our fists simply passed through each other.

Amy giggled.

Noah sighed. "Yeah, I never could get that to actually work in here."

"So . . . that's it?" asked Sam. She peered into the dark gym. "The T. rex isn't coming back?"

"No, this is where his program ends," replied Noah. "And he'll completely reset in a minute or so. I was thinking about making him play basketball when he's in the gym. But I ran out of time."

"That would've been funny," Amy said. "With those little arms."

"I know, right?" asked Noah. "I spent way too much time on him already, though."

"I can tell," I said. "Amazing detail."

"Thanks," Noah said. His avatar gave a polite bow.

Sam, Amy, and I just had the honor of being the first to test Noah's new virtual reality program. That's right—my best bud was a brilliant programmer. And for the past several months, he had been using every bit of his free time to create a virtual Swift Academy. Of course, he didn't have time to reproduce *every* classroom, but what he did create looked impressively accurate, right down to the smallest detail.

Noah even did a great job on our four avatars. Each of our characters looked lifelike—it seemed as if we were actually in the school's first-floor hallway when, in actuality, we were each in our own homes.

Noah created a system where we could put our phones in a special visor. Then we could connect to the program through Wi-Fi or our cell service. The program itself was on the school servers so we could log on and view the virtual world through our phones no matter where we were. Add a special controller for each hand and we could move our hands and pick up virtual items in his virtual school.

"You guys did great until the end there," Noah said.

"So you *were* spying on us," said Amy. "I knew it."

"Of course," Noah said. "I had to see how you would react."

"How did you do it?" Sam asked.

"The easiest way I could think of," Noah replied. His avatar's left hand reached over and touched his right hand, which probably meant that Noah was pushing a button on the controller in real life. Then Noah disappeared.

"Cool," said Amy.

"I can make my character invisible and intangible," Noah's disembodied voice explained. "But I can still pick stuff up." A road flare rose from the wooden box and seemed to float around by itself.

"Good way to cheat at hide-and-seek," Sam said. "What button makes you invisible?"

"Sorry," Noah said as he reappeared. "Only the creator has that power."

Sam's avatar shook her head. "Figures."

Amy's avatar looked to the left. "I have to go," she said. "My mother's calling me for dinner."

"I'd better be going too," Sam added. "Thanks for letting us try your program."

"Yes, thank you," Amy agreed. "It's really cool."

"I'm glad you liked it," Noah replied. His program wasn't sophisticated enough to relay facial expressions, but I could tell from the sound of his voice that he was grinning from ear to ear.

I raised my hand and my avatar gave them a wave. "See you tomorrow."

The girls waved back before their avatars faded to nothing.

"So you're going to turn it in to Mr. Varma tomorrow?" I asked Noah.

"Yeah," he replied. "Then I'm going to open-source it for everyone."

"Really?" I asked. "So anyone can change any part of it?"

"Just about," he replied. "They'll be able to customize their avatars, add characters, change the different environments, create side missions . . ."

"Wow," I said. "Do you have any idea what you'll be unleashing?"

Noah's avatar nodded. "I can't wait to see what people come up with. But don't worry. We'll still have the basement to ourselves. That's unchangeable."

"Cool," I said.

When Noah created the game, he had our four avatars spawn in the basement. And only the four of us had access to that part of the school. We even used the access code we already had memorized thanks to a previous . . . mishap involving drones and the FBI.

See? Things get weird in the real Swift Academy, not just the virtual one.

"And . . ." Noah said, his avatar raising both hands. "Now I'll finally be able to pull my weight with *our* two projects."

"Don't worry, I'll put you to work tomorrow," I said. "But first I have a question. . . . Will the T. rex chase you if you remain completely still, like in the movies?"

Noah's avatar raised his hands in an exaggerated shrug. "I guess you'll have to try and see."

"Let's do it!" I said, and I moved my avatar down the hall. Noah and I ran up the stairs to give the T. rex another try.

The Audible Escalation

"I CAN'T BELIEVE YOU LEFT ME ALL THE BORING busywork," Noah said as he glued another balsa wood tail fin onto a tiny rocket's fuselage.

"What was that?" I asked. "That didn't sound like, 'Thank you, Tom. Thanks for covering for me while I finished my virtual reality program.'"

"Thank you, Tom," Noah repeated in a mocking voice.

I gave a wide grin and shrugged. "No need to thank me. What are friends for?"

Noah shook his head and went back to his work. I

went back to measuring out chemicals and filling small rocket payload compartments.

Mr. Edge's engineering class was abuzz with activity as groups put the finishing touches on their projects. After all, today was the last working day before the big field trip. Every year, select students from the academy get to test some of their bigger inventions at a nearby summer camp. Camp Northwood is normally empty during the school year, so there's plenty of room to spread out.

But that wasn't all. Students from two other STEM schools are invited and everyone competes for a special grant. It's a great way to field-test some of our larger inventions as well as see what students from other schools have been up to.

Noah sighed. He was only halfway through installing tail fins for our project. We had twelve rockets total, and at three fins each, that's thirty-six fins. But wait, each rocket was a two-stage rocket. That's double the number of fins—seventy-two in all.

We had to make two-stage rockets to reach clouds at least as high as ten thousand feet (or 3,048 meters). Why must our rockets reach clouds, you may ask. It's because our project was about cloud seeding!

Cloud seeding is when people drop chemicals into clouds to make water droplets form, causing the natural phenomenon of precipitation . . . or, you know . . . rain. Now, this is usually done from a plane, but our project was going to use twelve model rockets set off one after another. It was going to be like the grand finale at a fireworks show . . . except it'd be in the daytime and they wouldn't explode.

"Excuse me," said Simone Mosby. She placed a tiny object onto the corner of our worktable. I squinted down at the object and saw it was a small square mirror on a tiny stand. "Try not to move this, please," she said as she crouched beside the table. Once eye-level with the mirror, she seemed to aim it like a tiny cannon.

"No problem," said Noah. "Nothing exciting going on over here."

That couldn't be said for the rest of the classroom. Everyone was preparing for the big field trip. Some were putting the finishing touches on their builds, like we were, while others were doing last-minute tests, like Simone. I watched as she placed tiny mirrors onto several other worktables around the room.

Simone's project was pretty cool. Her invention was

kind of a reverse laser microphone, and lasers always raise the cool factor for any invention. Now, laser microphones have been around for years. They are special devices that shoot a laser at a window and read the vibrations from the glass. That means it can hear anyone talking in that room. For Simone's project, she planned to use a powerful enough laser to transmit sound as well as receive it. If it worked, it would be a great way to communicate across line-of-sight distances in the event that all other forms of communication were cut off.

"All right," Simone said as she positioned the last mirror. "A little smoke, please."

Mia Trevino crouched behind her worktable. Her father works in special effects in movies, so she often brings fun devices to school. Today she operated one of her dad's smaller smoke machines. Mia pressed a button on the black box and a puff of smoke burst from the machine's nozzle. Mia used a clipboard to waft the smoke toward the center of the classroom. Soon, the entire room had a slight haze to it.

"That should do it," said Simone.

"Good," said Mia. "I'm still low on fluid, you know." She raised an eyebrow at the rest of the students. "Unless anyone wants to help me with that." No one responded.

Of course, she was talking about her missing gallons of fog fluid that someone had *borrowed* two days ago.

The missing fluid was the latest in a string of . . . mishaps . . . happening to many of the Swift Academy students. There were projects with missing components, disassembled devices, and even rewired mechanisms. No one knew who the prankster was but everyone was on guard, especially since we were so close to the field trip.

"Safety goggles on, everyone," Mr. Edge instructed. He pulled his goggles down from his forehead.

Those who weren't already wearing goggles did the same. Since there was no telling what students were up to in this class, everyone pretty much kept his or her goggles close at hand.

"Okay, nobody move, please," Simone said as she hovered over a black cylindrical device.

She flicked a toggle switch on the side of the device and a green beam appeared out of one end. Normally, laser beams are invisible to the naked eye, but this one reflected off Mia's smoke. The thin line crisscrossed all over the classroom as it bounced off the tiny mirrors placed about the room. Students backed away from the laser beam, careful not to block it.

"How long have you extended your beam with the mirrors?" Mr. Edge asked Simone.

"Approximately twenty-five meters," she replied. "I hope to double or even triple the distance during the field trip." She picked up a handheld mic and turned to the rest of the class. "Can someone help with the sound?"

"I'm in," Noah said as he scrambled to his feet. I got the feeling he wanted to put off some of his "boring busywork."

Simone handed Noah the microphone. "Can you stand outside the classroom?"

"You bet," he said as he snaked the cord past the students. He stepped outside and closed the door, careful to make sure the cord ran underneath.

Simone moved to the head of the classroom, where the beam ended on a tiny green dot on the wall, just above Mr. Edge's desk. Simone placed a thin piece of metal on a stand and slid it in front of the beam.

"Okay, Noah!" Simone shouted. "Say something."

Although Noah's words were muffled coming from the hallway, they were crystal clear coming from the sheet of metal. "Noah Newton on the mic," he said. "Step onto the dance floor!"

The class laughed.

Simone held a small device next to the metal. It was a decibel meter. It measured how loud sounds could be. "Fifty-three decibels," she announced, before replacing the metal with a thin sheet of wood. She turned toward the door. "Say it again, Noah."

"What do you want me to say?" Noah's voice emitted from the wood. It was quieter and muddier.

"You have to say the same exact thing," Simone said. "So I can get a precise reading."

"Noah Newton on the mic," he repeated. "Step onto the dance floor." Then he added a rhyme. "Not nearly as funny as it was before."

The class laughed again.

"Thirty-eight decibels," Simone reported. Then she replaced the wood with a pane of glass. "One more time, Noah."

There was no answer.

Actually, that wasn't true. I could hear Noah's muffled voice through the closed door but I couldn't hear his voice vibrating off the glass.

"Again, Noah?" Simone asked.

Once again, no sound emanated from the glass.

Simone reached out and angled it a bit and, for a split second there, I thought I heard a bit of Noah's voice before ...

POW!

The pane of glass shattered as if it had been filled with tiny explosives. Simone let out a short scream as she stumbled backward. I hopped off my stool and raced to the head of the class. Mr. Edge and I were the first ones there.

"Are you all right?" I asked.

"I'm okay," Simone replied. She was somewhat dazed but otherwise seemed fine. There was just a tiny nick on her left cheek, and a bead of blood began to form.

Mr. Edge pulled two tissues from a box on his desk and gently held them against her face. "Here, hold this," he instructed.

Simone took the tissues and Mr. Edge walked her toward the classroom door. "Let's get you to the school nurse," he said. "It just looks like a small nick, but it'll be best to have her take a look at you." He looked over his shoulder. "Tom, power down the laser. I'll call Mr. Jacobs to clean up the glass, so everyone be careful until he gets here."

I went over and switched off Simone's laser. Noah walked in as Mr. Edge and Simone left.

"What happened?" Noah asked.

"There was no sound at all," I replied. "And then the entire pane of glass exploded."

"That doesn't make sense," he said. "We saw her use the laser on glass last week. It worked just fine."

"Let's check it out," I said, leading the way to the front of the classroom. We knelt beside the pile of broken glass and I carefully picked up the biggest shard. Noah grabbed another.

"Looks like regular glass," Noah said.

My finger easily slid along the flat surface—too easily. The glass was coated with a slick, clear liquid.

"What is that?" I asked. "Grease?"

Noah rubbed his thumb and forefinger together and then smelled them. "I think so, yeah," he replied. "Why would Simone put grease on the glass?"

"Maybe she didn't," I suggested.

Noah raised an eyebrow. "Another prank?"

I shrugged. "Could be."

Noah grimaced and shook his head. "This is more than just a prank, man."

3

The Construction
Destruction

"WE HAVE TO HIDE OUR GEAR," NOAH SAID. "WE have to hide it while we're still here, and when we get to the camp . . . all the time."

"Everything's locked up in Mr. Edge's storeroom," I said. "No one has broken in there yet, right? I mean, Mia's fog fluid was just in the classroom when it was stolen, right?"

"That's what she said," Noah replied. He nodded down at the cardboard box he was carrying. "We should hide this stuff, too."

Noah and I were busy working on the next project for

the field trip. Okay, maybe it wasn't an official project but it was just as important. You see, every year, at the end of the summer camp field trip, all three schools get together for an official unofficial water balloon battle. Right now we were on our way to the gym to test our contribution to the war effort.

There were a lot of students roaming the halls during class. Luckily, many of the teachers were a little lenient with the students participating in the upcoming field trip. Our physics teacher, Mrs. Lee, was no exception. Of course, both of our projects very much involved physics.

We entered the gym to see the place buzzing with more students than usual. It seems we weren't the only ones with the idea to test our invention in the large space. However, there was one invention that had taken up residence in the gym for the past couple of weeks, and that was Evan Wittman's Christmas tree.

"If that thing works, it's going to win for sure," Noah said.

"No doubt," I agreed.

Evan's invention wasn't really a Christmas tree. It just looked a lot like one—an upside-down Christmas tree. It was a special design to help pull water from the air.

24

You know how dew can cover everything, early in the morning? Well, Evan's tree was designed to collect that dew on its tiny branches. The branches were angled so the water could run down toward the bigger branches, which were connected to the four main "trunks" that supported the whole tree. Then all the water got collected in a container in the middle of the trunks.

Evan had been assembling it for the past two weeks. Now it looked as if he and Kent Jackson were taking it apart and packing it up for the field trip. Evan stood on a tall ladder and pulled out a small branch from one of the four trunks.

"There's room over here," I said. I nodded at an empty space near the bleachers.

Noah and I set our boxes down at the base of the bleachers and began to unpack them. I pulled out my old paintball gun and screwed on the air tank. Then I attached the PVC barrel we had designed just for this project. Paintball guns had oversize parts to begin with, so this longer, fatter barrel looked like an exaggerated silencer. I felt like a hit man in a spy thriller.

I grinned at Noah. "The name is Swift. Tom Swift."

Noah rolled his eyes and finished unpacking his box.

He pulled out several paper cylinders and laid them out on the bottom bleacher.

"Cool VR program, Noah," Ashley Robbins said as she and Jenna Davis walked over.

"Thanks," replied Noah.

Ashley grinned. "That T. rex was superscary!"

"Hey." Jenna pointed at the cylinders on the bleacher. "I thought your project involved rockets."

"It does," said Noah. "These are for the battle royale at the end."

"The water balloon fight?" Jenna asked. "Cool! What are you going to do?"

"You know those T-shirt guns they use at ball games?" I asked. "The ones that shoot rolled-up shirts into the crowd using air pressure?"

"Oh, yeah," replied Jenna.

"Well, picture that but with a water balloon," I said.

Ashley cocked her head. "How are you going to do that?" she said. "Won't the water balloon break when you hit it with all that air pressure?"

"That was my question," Noah replied.

I picked up one of the paper cylinders from the bleacher. "So we designed these little shuttles. They're sturdy enough to cradle the water balloon inside the barrel." I flapped the shuttle up and down. "But light enough to fall away from the water balloon in flight."

"Theoretically," Noah added.

"Theoretically," I agreed.

"You're going to test it in here?" asked Jenna.

"Sorta," I replied. "We want to try out the shuttle with no wind to see if it'll work."

Noah pulled out a small blue beanbag. "And we're starting with these."

I nodded at Jenna. "You came up with the shoe charger, right?"

She nodded. "That's me."

In engineering class, Jenna talked about converting a pair of hiking boots with a device that charged a battery as you walked. That way your phone would never be in danger of dying. She described it as the same principle used for flashlights you charge by either cranking or squeezing a lever.

Noah pointed at her. "Say, has anyone tried to mess with your boots? Trying to prank you or anything?"

Jenna shook her head. "No. But I don't know how they could. I take them with me everywhere I go."

We looked down to notice the large brown hiking boots on her feet.

"Hey, nice," Noah said. "The heel is a little thicker, but other than that, they look perfectly normal."

"Thanks." Jenna grinned. "I'm going to be hiking all weekend, which is something I like to do anyway. It's a win-win."

Ashley and Jenna stuck around while we finished setting up our makeshift T-shirt/beanbag launcher. When the air pressure was adjusted, Noah loaded the wide PVC barrel with one of the beanbag shuttle combos.

Once we were good to go, I aimed the barrel up toward a section of empty bleachers. "Fire in the hole," I said, and pulled the trigger.

FOOMP!

The shuttle worked just as expected. It stayed with the beanbag for about two meters before the wind resistance reached its peak. The shuttle fell away, and the beanbag thumped onto higher bleachers.

"Cool," said Jenna. "Can I try?"

"Sure," I said. I glanced at Noah and he gave me a nod of approval.

Noah loaded another beanbag into a shuttle and

handed it over. I carefully slid them into the oversize barrel and handed the launcher to Jenna. She aimed it toward the bleachers, then stopped. She brought it back down and turned it sideways.

"Is this the switch?" she asked, tapping at the converted trigger.

"Careful where you aim . . . ," Noah began.

FOOMP!

The beanbag shot out of the barrel and flew toward Evan's Christmas tree.

Jenna yipped in surprise, her eyes widening. She thrust the launcher back into my hands. "Sorry, sorry!"

Luckily, the beanbag narrowly missed the inverted tree. It sailed past and smacked against the wall beside it.

"Hey!" Evan shouted.

I glanced over at Jenna and then realized that she and Ashley had already backed several feet away. I was left holding the bag—or holding the launcher, rather.

"Sorry!" I shouted back to Evan. "A little misfire." I turned to the girls. "You owe me one," I said.

They were gone.

"Oh, yeah," Noah said with a laugh. "They totally left you hanging."

I sighed. "How about we go outside to finish testing this?"

"Good idea," Noah said. He nodded toward Evan and his tree. "You going to do the walk of shame and get our beanbag back?"

"Me?" I asked.

"Dude. You let her shoot it," Noah said.

I shook my head and set the launcher down on the bleachers. Then I took a deep breath and casually strolled across the gym, trying not to look too embarrassed.

When I got to Evan's area, he was climbing up the ladder to remove another branch.

"Sorry again," I told him.

"That's okay," Evan replied. "You didn't hit—"

CRACK!

Something snapped at the base of the tree and the whole thing began to fall over.

"Oh no, no, no, no!" Evan shouted as he reached for the nearest branch. He latched on to the branch, but since they were meant to be removable, it pulled out from the trunk. The tree toppled over onto the hard gym floor. Several branches shattered under the weight.

Noah led the way as everyone in the gym ran up to the crash site. "Aw, man," Noah said. "Did our beanbag do that?"

Evan shook his head. "No, it missed it completely. I don't understand." He got on his hands and knees and examined the base of the tree. I got down on the ground with him.

Evan's tree normally sat on four main trunks, attached to a thick base. Now that the tree was on its side, only four stumps jutted up from the base. Two of the stumps were splintered where the main break occurred. The other two had clean cuts.

I pointed to the cuts. "Are they supposed to be like that?"

"No way," Evan replied.

"Was there a flaw in the plastic?" I asked. "Something that would make them separate like that?"

Evan shook his head. "Not at all." He reached out and touched the edges. "Do you see that? Someone cut this."

"Hey, what's that?" asked Noah. He had come down to the floor with us and pointed to a dark stain on the green trunk. He smeared it with his finger and then pulled away. His finger was bright red. He gave it a brief sniff. "That's blood. Look's like someone got a little instant karma and cut themselves."

Evan got to his feet. He didn't seem to care.

Noah and I joined him as he surveyed the wreckage. "Will you be able to repair it by tomorrow?"

Evan sighed. "I think so. Maybe after an all-nighter."

I winced. I've pulled a few all-nighters myself working on projects. Luckily, those all-nighters weren't because someone had vandalized one of my inventions. And let's be honest, that's what this was—vandalism. This went way past simple pranks.

Noah caught my eye and nodded. "I'm serious, man," he said. "We have to hide our stuff."

The Inappropriate
Appropriation

"THERE WAS AIDEN WILSON'S WATER FILTER,"
Noah added. "Remember how it grew mold a couple of
days ago? He'll be lucky to have it cleaned and rebuilt
by tomorrow."

I finished filling another water balloon and handed
it to Noah. "Yeah, but you really think someone planted
mold?" I asked as I wrapped the mouth of the next balloon around the spigot. I slowly opened the valve, filling
another balloon with water.

Noah tied off the balloon and placed it with the

others. "It's possible. And very difficult to prove. I mean, who plants mold?"

Okay, that one seemed kind of unlikely, but there was certainly evidence now that someone was doing more than just pranking the students' projects.

"But why would someone want to sabotage people's inventions?" I asked. "I mean, we're mainly competing against other schools, not each other."

Noah shrugged. "Bragging rights? I don't know."

We finished filling up our water balloons from the spigot outside the school. Noah carried the five balloons in a plastic grocery bag, while I hauled the launcher. Now we just needed a place to test it.

The grounds behind the academy were the perfect place to test things like this. Other than the running track and small set of bleachers, the campus was wide open. A few groves with trees and bushes dotted the large manicured landscape. There were plenty of places to launch our balloons, but there were too many targets running about. And by targets, I mean fellow academy students.

Some were testing their projects for the upcoming field trip—Steve Krieger and Asia Astra were flying a drone in one of the open areas. Other students were on free periods and took the opportunity to get some fresh air while they studied. There were some people sitting under trees wearing VR headsets. Obviously even more students were enjoying Noah's VR program.

That was weird—going outside the school to run around inside the school . . . virtually.

"How about those trees?" Noah asked. He pointed to a clump of trees and bushes about twenty meters away.

"Target acquired," I said objectively. I readied the launcher.

Noah placed a water balloon inside a paper shuttle, then gently slid the entire package into the PVC barrel. I aimed the launcher at the small grove and fired.

FOOMP!

The shuttle worked perfectly. The balloon fired out of the tube without breaking. But unfortunately, the balloon fell short of the target. It splattered on the ground about three meters in front of the nearest bush.

"I'm dialing up the PSI," I said as I turned a thumbscrew on the back of the launcher.

Noah placed the next package into the tube and

stepped back. "I'll wait over here," he said. "Just in case that's too *much* pressure."

"Thanks for your support," I said bracingly.

Noah shrugged. "Hey, next time I'll bring a poncho and stand as close as you like."

I aimed the launcher at the tree and pulled the trigger.

FOOMP!

That water balloon didn't break as it exited the barrel either. It soared over the field and struck one of the trees dead center.

SPLAT!

The balloon exploded on impact.

"Hey!" a voice shouted. There was a scuffle, and then we saw Amy peek out from behind the tree.

"Whoa, sorry!" I shouted. "We didn't know anyone was there."

Noah and I grabbed our gear and ran up to the small grove. As we neared, I saw that Amy wasn't alone.

"What are you two doing here?" Noah asked.

"Trying to find a secluded place for our field test," Sam replied. "Somewhere we won't get splattered by water balloons."

"How were we supposed to know you were hiding over here?" Noah asked defensively.

"We're not hiding," Amy said. She gave a slight cringe. "Okay, we're hiding a little."

"So, now that we uncovered your secret testing site, are you going to finally tell us about your project?" I asked.

Sam and Amy glanced at each other.

"Come on," Noah urged. "The field trip's tomorrow. That's only a day to keep the secret."

The four of us collaborated on inventions all the time, but Sam and Amy had been tight-lipped about their project for weeks. They had both weighed in on our cloud-seeding rockets and even our water balloon launcher. But all the while, they didn't give us a hint as to what their invention was about. It was very strange and a little unfair.

The girls glanced back at each other. Sam shrugged. "All right." She held up a finger. "But no jokes, jabs, or ribbing." She aimed her finger at Noah. "I'm looking at you, Noah Newton."

Noah raised his hands. "Hey. It's me."

Sam nodded. "Don't I know it."

Amy rolled her eyes. "Come on." She waved us forward as she disappeared into the grove.

Noah and I set our gear down and followed Amy in. Sam brought up the rear. My eyes darted around the area, anxious for the first glimpse of the mystery project.

They led us to a weird contraption. Two white pipes jutted straight out of a small hole in the ground, rotating around each other as one spewed out a thin trail of soil. The pipes had a ring of soil around them, so it looked as if it had been doing this for a while. Two thin wires led away from the device.

I leaned out of the grove, visually tracing the wires. They ran to a set of solar panels on the ground.

"Your invention digs a water well," I said. "And it's solar-powered. Very cool."

"Fully automated," Sam said proudly. "It's slow, but you could theoretically have several going at once."

"How are you going to fit a bucket down there?" Noah asked.

Sam gave Noah a shove on the arm. "It's not that kind of well. When it reaches the water table, you add a small pipe and pump the water out."

Noah shook his head. "Wait, hold up, hold up . . . I

don't get it. I thought you *didn't* want people to call you Water Girl."

Sam had that nickname tied around her neck when she had first started at the academy. She had received a full scholarship after creating a big water-sourcing project. It was so big that it remained top secret since it was optioned by a corporation that wanted to test it across the globe.

How do a bunch of twelve- and thirteen-year-olds react to that? They nickname her Water Girl.

"Noah," Sam warned.

Noah raised his hands in defense. "I'm just asking."

"Well, it kinda just came to me," Sam explained. "And it would mesh perfectly with my other invention."

"Which you still can't tell us about," I added.

"Right," Sam agreed. "And Amy had some great ideas for increasing the efficiency and reducing real-world production costs."

Amy looked away, tucking a piece of hair behind her ear. "Not really."

Noah shook his head. "And we still can't call you Water Girl, huh?"

"Why do you think we've been keeping everything

top secret?" Sam asked with a frown. "So I wouldn't get lip from people like you."

"I guess that makes sense," I said with a shrug.

"I thought you were hiding from the vandal," Noah said.

"What do you mean?" asked Amy.

Noah and I recapped our conversation about all the sabotaged projects.

"Planting mold?" Sam asked with a raised eyebrow. "Really? I'm all for a good conspiracy theory, but this one seems out there."

I folded my arms and nodded toward Sam. "I don't know, Noah. You think she's trying to throw us off the scent?"

"What do you mean?" Noah asked.

"Sam is definitely the vandal," I said. "She doesn't want anyone to take away her inventor cred."

Sam shook her head while Amy covered her mouth and giggled quietly.

Noah's eyes widened and a devious grin stretched across his face. He pointed to the bandage on one of Sam's fingers. "See, she even cut herself when she sawed through Evan's project!"

Sam rolled her eyes. "Like half the students don't have bandages on their fingers." She grinned up at me. "You'll have to do better than that, Swift."

"What about the grease on her shirt?" I asked. "That could be the same grease that messed up Simone's laser transmitter."

Noah rubbed his chin thoughtfully. "Excellent deduction, Holmes."

Sam sighed. "Yeah, no one has grease on his or her shirt around here either." She held out her wrists as if she were about to be handcuffed. "All right. You got me," she said sarcastically. "I've been going around and messing up everyone's projects."

Amy laughed harder.

"You have?" asked a voice behind me. I spun around to see Jenna Davis standing there.

"What? No," I said. "We were just joking."

"Oh," Jenna said. Then she leaned past me to look at Sam and Amy's well digger. "Is this your project?" she asked.

As Amy and Sam discussed their project with Jenna (and Sam doesn't stop once she gets going), Noah and I had the same idea—slowly back out of there and return to our testing. I caught Sam's eye before we left. Her lips tightened and she shook her head ever so slightly. She didn't have to say it out loud. Her look translated what she wanted to say loud and clear.

"Thanks a lot, Swift."

5

The Coloration Recommendation

"IT'LL BE GOOD TO GET YOU OUTDOORS FOR A weekend," my dad said. "And not be locked in your room with a VR headset on." He nodded at Noah. "I'm assuming the same for you?"

"Yes, sir," Noah replied. "And whatever screen time Tom does, double it for me."

"Triple it," I corrected.

Noah had come home with me for dinner and to help finish up our projects for the big field trip. We still had more fins to glue and more balloon launchers to make, so after dinner, we worked atop the large work-table in our garage. My dad kept us company as he finished his coffee, which he drank from his favorite mug. It was one of my first inventions—a mug with a built-in thermometer. It told the temperature of the liquid inside, in both Fahrenheit and Celsius.

We had to put in some late hours because I had expanded our project somewhat. See, since we were launching twelve rockets for our cloud-seeding project, I wondered why we couldn't do the same for the water balloons. By the time school dismissed, I had sketched out a design for a manifold that would direct the air to one of twelve different PVC barrels. That way we could launch one balloon right after another.

My dad sipped his cup of coffee as he watched me work. "So, let me get this straight. You haven't completed your main project for school, yet you're working on your water balloon launcher?"

Noah and I glanced at each other. "Sounds right," I said.

"That about sums it up," Noah added.

"Besides, we're practically finished with our rockets," I said. "Well, Noah is."

My dad took another sip of coffee. "What color are you going to paint your rockets?"

"We don't have time to paint them," I said. "Besides, their color won't affect their function."

"I see," my dad replied.

I knew that tone. His "I see" really meant: I see *what you missed there.*

I sighed. "Okay, what is it?" I asked. "What did we forget?"

My father took another sip and shrugged. "Well, I can think of two reasons why you should paint your rockets."

Noah put aside the fuselage he had been working on. "I want to hear this," he said.

"The first reason is a simple sense of pride," my father explained. "It shows that your project is complete. Someone may think, 'If they didn't have time to paint their work, where else did they cut corners?'"

Noah pointed at me. "That's what I told him."

"You're right," I said, and nodded. "And that's great and everything. But we don't have time to paint all the rockets *and* finish the water balloon launcher."

My dad raised an eyebrow.

"And . . . ," I added before he could get a word in. "Even though the water balloon battle isn't an official competition, what about the pride in coming up with inventive new ways to soak people?"

"That's right," Noah agreed. "Swift Academy has to represent."

My dad chuckled. "I'll give you that. But you didn't ask about the other reason for painting your rockets."

I winced a bit. This was going to hurt.

"And that is?" I asked.

"Well, how hard is it going to be to locate and recover twelve cardboard rockets in a wooded area?" he asked.

I groaned.

Model rockets weren't like fireworks; they didn't just explode after you shot them into the air. After they ejected the chemicals into the clouds, the rockets would fall back to the earth with tiny parachutes.

"Twenty-four," Noah corrected. "These are two-stage rockets, so there would be twenty-four pieces to recover. The twelve rockets plus each of their booster sections."

I groaned louder.

The boosters were smaller sections at the base of the rockets that contained their very own engines. It would be the first engine to ignite and lift the rocket only so far. After burning through all its fuel, it would then ignite the engine just above it, in the main section of the rocket, after which the booster and spent engine would fall away. The booster was so small and light that it wouldn't need its own parachute.

It didn't really matter which parts needed parachutes and which didn't. They would all fall back to Earth and we'd have to locate all twenty-four of them—not only are they reusable, but to not pick them up would be littering.

I lowered my wrench. "All right. I guess the multiple balloon launcher is out."

"Now hang on," my dad said. He put his mug down and opened a nearby cabinet. "I think I have some quick-drying stuff in here." He rummaged around until he pulled out two cans of spray paint. "Here are two colors that aren't found in nature. Which will it be? Neon green or hot pink?"

Noah and I glanced at each other. "Neon green," we said in unison.

Noah shrugged. "Although pink would be easier to spot in the woods."

"And Sam got a new nickname just for coming up with a water invention," I countered. "What kind of nickname do you think we'd get?"

Noah's brow furrowed. "Oh."

"Neon green it is," my dad said as he put back the pink can. The remaining can clacked loudly as he shook it. "Now, before giving up on the launcher, let me ask you this. . . . Is there a rule against having an assistant help you finish your project?"

Noah and I glanced at each other again. "No," we said in unison, both of us smiling.

"Okay then," my dad said as he pressed the garage door button. The large door slowly rumbled open. Still shaking the can, he snatched up two of the completed rockets and took them toward the driveway. "Make sure the Swift Academy students are the driest ones this weekend," he said. "After your rain project, of course."

The Transportation Speculation

THE BUS HIT A BUMP ON THE GRAVEL ROAD AND my finger slid across my tablet. Now my new go-cart design looked as if it had a long antenna extending from the middle of the front seat. I shut off my tablet and tucked it into my backpack. I stared out the bus window, watching the thick woods go by.

I guess I could've just as easily used pen and paper to draw my design. Sam had warned me about bringing too many electronics. But hey, it wasn't as if we were headed out to the wilderness. I watched more of the dark forest go by. Okay, so maybe we *were* kind of headed out into the wilderness. But the summer camp had nice cabins with electricity and even Wi-Fi. Besides, we weren't going there for the whole summer-camp experience. This was just for the weekend.

Noah plopped back into the seat beside me. We weren't supposed to be out of our seats while the bus was moving, but some of the students got away with it.

"Okay, we're in big trouble," he said in a low voice. "And by *we* I mean *you*."

"What are you talking about?" I asked.

"I just talked to Chris Hibbard and he told me about this rumor going around," Noah replied.

I shook my head. "What rumor?"

Noah lowered his voice even more. "The rumor that Sam has been vandalizing everyone's projects."

"What?" I glanced ahead. Sam and Amy sat in the seat directly in front of us. "Who started that rumor?" I asked in a whisper.

"I'm guessing you did," Noah replied. "Remember? Yesterday, outside the school?"

"That was a joke," I said. I tapped him on the chest. "A joke you helped with, by the way."

"I know," Noah said. "And that's what I told Chris.

But I don't know how many other people have heard it."

My lips tightened as I shook my head. "Jenna must've said something to someone."

"We told her it was a joke too," Noah added and then raised his eyebrows. "Man, Sam is going to kill you."

"Me?!" I said. "We were *all* joking about it!"

"Yeah, but you started it, remember?" Noah asked.

I stood and scanned the rest of the bus passengers. "I have to find Jenna and tell her to cool it with all the rumors." I looked behind me, but I didn't spot her anywhere. Up ahead, I just saw the backs of everyone's heads.

I slid out from our seat and moved up the aisle. Hopefully, I could at least get to Jenna before Sam found out about the rumors. She was one of my best friends in the whole world but honestly, Sam could be scary sometimes.

"Remain seated while the bus is moving," the bus driver announced. I locked eyes with him in the long rearview mirror above the windshield. He shook his head slightly.

I immediately backtracked to my seat.

Noah laughed. "Busted."

"I don't see her anywhere," I reported. "Do you think she might've skipped?"

Noah shook his head. "No way. I saw her helping load the truck before we left."

Since so much equipment had to be transported, there was a large panel truck following our bus. It was full of everyone's components, tools, and even luggage for the weekend.

"Nice one, Swift," Sam said from the seat in front of us. "I see you haven't perfected your stealthy ninja skills yet."

"Not yet," I agreed.

Good. The news hadn't made its way to Sam yet. I could enjoy a little more time being her friend before she disowned me.

I settled back into my seat and tried to enjoy the rest of the trip. I watched the trees go by and did my best not to worry about the rumor spreading like a zombie outbreak.

Before long, we turned a tight corner and the main entrance came into view. Two large poles flanked the road, with a sign between them that read WELCOME TO CAMP NORTHWOOD. The bus trundled under the sign as we drove into the camp.

I leaned over the seatback in front of me. "Pretty cool, huh?"

"I don't know," Sam said. "All I see are a bunch of trees."

I nodded. "Yeah?"

"My well dig—" She stopped herself and glanced around. "My *invention* doesn't do well with tree roots or rocky soil."

"Oh." I looked out the window. "I'm sure there'll be plenty of clearings to choose from."

"That's what I told her," Amy agreed. She was busy putting on sunblock.

"We're going to need one too," I added. "Model rockets and trees don't mix."

Then I noticed that Amy spread sunscreen all over her watch. "Uh, you got some on your watch, Amy." The square device actually looked like a smart watch with a blank screen.

"I know," Amy said as she continued to apply lotion. "And it's not a watch. That is my UV detector."

"What's that?" I asked.

"You know the film badges that change color if a person is accidentally exposed to too much radiation?" she asked.

"Dosimeters?" I asked. "The kind of badges people wear at nuclear power plants?"

"Exactly," Amy replied. "Well, this works on the same principle, but it's set up to detect too much UV radiation." She held up the tube of sunblock. "That's why I have to give it the same protection I'm getting, so I can get an accurate reaction."

"Very cool invention, Ames," Noah chimed in as he leaned forward to get a better look. "Is that an extra-credit sort of thing?"

Amy shook her head. "No, it's a not-getting-skin-cancer sort of thing."

Amy seemed surprised when Sam, Noah, and I laughed. I don't think she meant to make a joke. Her face flushed a bit before she joined in.

After the bus pulled to a stop in the camp's large parking lot, everyone stood, shuffled down the main aisle, and exited the bus. From the look of things, it appeared that the Swift Academy students were the last to arrive. Two other large charter buses were already there, with two other panel trucks. Students and teachers from the other schools were already milling about and unloading their gear.

Each group wore matching T-shirts, so it was easy to tell which students belonged to each school. The Swift Academy students all wore yellow shirts with the academy logo plastered across the front. The students from the Bradley Institute wore bright green shirts while the Liniford STEM school students wore blue shirts. As the students mingled, the colors swirled like a hydrothermal chemistry experiment.

I snapped out of my daze when I realized that I had better find Jenna before everyone swirled together too much. I honed in on all the yellow shirts and scanned everyone as quickly as I could. Luckily, I spotted Jenna in the cargo truck. She was already there, helping people unload their projects.

"Hey, Jenna." I ran up to the ramp. "Can I talk to you for a second?"

"Okay," she said, looking a little confused. She walked down the ramp and joined me at the side of the truck.

"Did you happen to tell anyone that Sam has been sabotaging people's projects?" I asked.

Jenna wrinkled her brow and shook her head. "No." Then her eyes widened. "I did tell Ashley that you were joking about it. But there's no way she took me seriously."

"Maybe she did," I said. I told her about the rumor Noah had heard.

Jenna brought her hands to her mouth. "Oh no!" she said. "If she's telling people that, I'll tell her to stop right away." She shook her head. "I'm so sorry, Tom."

"It's okay," I said. "You know how these things can start."

Jenna rolled her eyes. "Don't I know it." She turned and disappeared into the multicolored crowd.

As soon as she was gone, Noah appeared. "Well?"

"It was her, all right," I said. "Well, her and Ashley. But Jenna's going to take care of it."

"I hope so," Noah said, shaking his head. "Because I'd hate to be you if this thing gets back to Sam."

"I'd hate to be me, too," I agreed.

We both talked big, but I'm sure Sam would understand if she ever did find out. It might take a while, but she gets how things can be taken out of context.

Honestly, I was more worried about how the rumor would affect her confidence. Samantha Watson was probably one of the smartest students at Swift Academy. But most of the time, her confidence level is the polar opposite of her IQ. She is constantly trying to prove herself to everyone around her, and holds herself to an impossible standard. If this rumor got back to her, she'd be crushed.

Noah dusted off his hands. "Now that that's settled, let's get our gear."

"I think we just have to unload it," I said. "They are supposed to have someone . . ."

"Welcome to camp . . . *Junior*," interrupted a familiar voice.

My shoulders tightened at the sound of that voice. There was only one person in the world who called me *Junior*. Well, two people, actually. There was also my dad's sister, Aunt Susan. But *Junior* doesn't sound like a derogatory name when she says it. No, only one person calls me Junior with the transparent delight of knowing that it really, really bugs me.

I turned around to see my old nemesis, Andrew Foger.

7

The Nemesis Resurgence

"JUNIOR?" NOAH ASKED WITH A WIDE GRIN. "OH man. I'm *so* using that."

"Hey, Andrew," I said, trying my best to hide my annoyance. I even forced a weak smile. "I didn't know you'd be here."

"What you don't know can fill a stadium, Junior," Andrew said with a laugh. He hadn't changed much. He was still larger than me, and stockier, and his bushy blond hair was as much of a bird's nest as ever. Even his half snarl, half grin was exactly the same. "I'm at Bradley now," he said proudly. "My dad's a major shareholder."

I ignored the stadium dig and nodded at Noah. "Noah, this is Andrew. Our dads used to work together."

Andrew snorted. "His dad used to work for mine, actually."

Actually that wasn't true (although I don't doubt Andrew saw it that way). Mr. Foger was a silent partner at one of my father's first companies. He was a banker who put up the capital while my father had the ideas. So, yeah, in a sense, Mr. Foger paid for everything while my father did all the work.

Either way you look at it, Andrew and I used to hang out a lot while our fathers took meetings, drew up business plans, and sometimes bickered over what direction the company should take.

Andrew was a year older so he always acted like the world's worst big brother. Not only would he talk me into doing crazy, sometimes dangerous things, he would also make it so I took the blame whenever we were caught. I don't know if it was the stress of starting a new company or all the mischief Andrew and I would get in, but my dad was not a happy camper back then.

When my father and Mr. Foger parted ways, I never expected to see Andrew again.

Andrew jutted a thumb at me. "So, what's Junior's big project this year?" he asked Noah.

"Actually, we have a cloud-seeding project," Noah replied.

Andrew nodded. "Not bad. Not bad," he said. "Not original, but not bad."

I shook my head. "Whatever." I started to walk away but Noah grabbed my arm.

"Wait a minute," Noah said to Andrew. "If you're so special, what's your project, then?"

"That's for me to know and you to find out," I muttered under my breath.

Andrew took in a deep breath. "That's for me to know and you to find out," he said proudly. Then he guffawed at his own punch line.

Andrew might've gotten a little taller, maybe a little wider, but he *really* hadn't changed much.

This time I grabbed Noah's arm and led him away. "Glad you asked?"

Noah shook his head. "Don't worry, man," he said. "I will *not* call you Junior."

"Thanks, dude," I said.

"Can I have your attention, please?" asked a tall

man in a brown shirt. He had gray-speckled hair and a friendly smile. Once the conversations died down he gazed out at the students and teachers. "My name is Tom Alexander, owner of Camp Northwood. I want to welcome everyone here and I hope your weekend is filled with discovery, innovation, and invention!"

There was a light smattering of applause.

"Now, you'll notice that my counselors are handing out maps," he continued. "These will direct you to your schools' cabins."

Some older kids, also in brown shirts, handed out maps to everyone. When I got mine, I opened it up to see the entire campgrounds laid out before me. There was a main road that ran down the middle of the camp, toward the lake. Several hiking trails branched off the road, leading to different clusters of cabins. It looked as if the Swift Academy male students had the longest hike. Our cabins were on the other side of the lake, so we had to trek to the end of the road and cross a bridge over a small inlet to get there.

"Don't worry about your luggage and your gear," Mr. Alexander continued. "Just group everything together and our counselors will make sure it gets to your cabins before you know it."

I glanced around and saw that the counselors were doing just that. Several older boys and girls loaded backpacks, trunks, and plastic bins onto low trailers. Once the trailers were full, electric golf carts would quietly haul them down the main road and out of sight.

"You have your maps, so have fun exploring the camp for a few hours," Mr. Alexander said. "Then everyone meet in the chow hall for lunch."

The giant herd of color-differentiated kids slowly broke up as everyone organized his or her gear. Noah and I put our backpacks onto the large plastic bins that held our rockets and balloon launchers. After that, we fell into step with the students walking down the main road.

We quickly caught up to Amy and Sam. They had the map spread open, gesturing to various points of interest.

"What about here?" asked Amy. She pointed to a large field beside an illustration of a swimming pool.

"Too public," Sam said. "I bet everyone who needs an open space will flock to that area. Besides, it doesn't have to be that big."

I looked over their shoulders. "There's some kind of

field near our cabins," I said. "That might work for our rockets and your digger."

Sam cocked her head. "Could be."

"We can check it out and let you know," Noah suggested.

"Okay," said Sam. "Shoot us a text."

"If you can get a signal," Amy said. "One of the Bradley students said the cell coverage is very spotty out here."

"Okay, then let me ask you this," Noah said with a grin. "Did you bring your VR gear?"

Amy smiled and nodded. "Oh yes."

Sam rolled her eyes. "Yeah, I couldn't resist either."

I spread my arms wide. "All of this nature around you and you want to spend your time glued to a screen?" I asked. "And not only that, but in a virtual version of our school? A place we get to escape for a few days?"

"I haven't had a chance to see the new program since Noah showed us the other day," Sam admitted. "And I hear that a bunch of people are already making cool changes."

"Once we set up our project, it takes care of itself," Amy added. "We can check it out then."

"The reason I ask," Noah continued, "is if the cell coverage is so bad, we can all use the camp's Wi-Fi to log on to my VR school. Then we can leave each other messages in the basement."

"Why not just send an e-mail?" I asked.

Noah shook his head. "Because leaving a message in the basement is way cooler."

Sam and Amy peeled off onto one of the trails with the rest of the girls from Swift Academy. We kept moving with our little pack down the main road, toward the lake.

"Hey, Junior," came Andrew's voice from behind us.

I sighed and glanced at Noah. He rolled his eyes.

I looked back to see Andrew Foger walking several paces behind us. He had two other Bradley students with him. And they were all blinding in their bright green T-shirts.

Was this guy following me just to be a pain? When I first looked over the map, I saw that the Bradley Institute students were placed at the other side of the camp. So there was no reason for them to be trailing behind the Swift Academy boys.

I stopped and turned to face him. "What do you want, Andrew?"

Andrew and the two boys caught up to us. As they approached, I saw that Andrew's friends were identical twins. They were both tall and thin and had long dark hair.

"This is Mike and Mark," Andrew said.

Noah and I introduced ourselves. The twins didn't say anything; they simply nodded.

"What do you want?" I repeated.

Andrew pointed past us. "I just thought I'd show you my project. You're about to pass it anyway."

The three Bradley students moved past us and continued down the road. Noah shrugged, and we followed them.

We crested a hill and saw a large rectangular structure on the side of the road. As we moved closer, I realized that it was a huge shipping container, like the kind you see stacked all over those big cargo ships.

"Check it," said Andrew. "My dad had a guy truck it in this morning." He spread his arms wide. "The Foger Survival Cabin. It's portable, securable, and completely off the grid." He sounded like a used-car salesman.

But I had to admit that I was impressed. The long metal box was painted dark green and had two windows cut into the side. The other thing that made it different from regular cargo containers was the row of large solar panels angled along the roof. There was even a satellite dish up there.

"You can keep the entire structure secure until you need it," Andrew said as he approached the end of the container. He unlatched the two industrial doors on the end and swung them open. Recessed about two meters inside the container was a wall with another door, except this looked like a regular house door, with a window and everything.

Andrew kicked at some empty cardboard boxes beside the door. "Excuse the mess. We're still installing some components," he said as he opened the door and went inside. Noah and I followed him and the twins.

"This is cool," Noah said as he looked around.

"I know, right?" asked Andrew.

The inside of the container looked like a regular house. A small kitchenette was on one end while the other end was dominated by a couch and a huge flat-screen television. In between, there were three beds, shelves of movies, and video-game consoles.

"You guys are staying here?" asked Noah.

"Beats staying in a musty cabin," said Mike or Mark.

I hated to admit it, but this was a great project. It was made by using a recycled shipping container and seemed very green all around—minus some of the creature comforts, of course.

"Very nice, Andrew," I admitted. "And completely off the grid?"

"You didn't see any wires, did you?" Andrew pointed to the ceiling. "Plus satellite Internet access."

"Probably faster than the Wi-Fi they have around here," added Mark. Or was it Mike?

"How many kilowatts do the solar panels generate?" I asked.

Andrew's brow furrowed. "Enough to get the job done."

"No, seriously," I continued. "How much power would you say this setup draws in one day?"

Andrew crossed his arms. "If you want to know the specs you'll have to buy one once they go into mass production." He turned to the twins and smiled. "My dad says we'll make a killing with all the tiny-house suckers." There were fist bumps all around.

And on that note, it was time to go.

"Well, thanks for showing us," I said, moving toward the door.

"Stop by anytime," Andrew sneered.

Noah and I stepped outside and continued up the main road.

"Dude," Noah said. "That kinda blows our project away."

"I think that was the point of that whole demonstration," I said. "But don't fall for it. I guarantee that he didn't hammer one nail in building that thing."

"What do you mean?" asked Noah.

"He and his dad always pay other people to do all their work for them," I said. "And you heard him in there. It's all about making money, not about helping people or making a cool discovery." I shook my head. "It sounds like neither one of them has changed a bit."

We continued down the road, putting Andrew Foger's cabin literally and figuratively behind us.

By the time Noah and I made it to our own cabin, all of our gear had been delivered. And it turned out that we shared our cabin with Terry Stephenson and Toby Nguyen. The place was basically one big room with a small bed on each wall. Terry and Toby's bins were already stowed next to their beds. Our gear was still in the center of the room. Of course, when we walked in, our cabinmates didn't even notice. They each sat on their beds wearing VR headgear.

I jutted a thumb at them. "I see the Wi-Fi works."

Noah threw his backpack onto his bed and rummaged through it. "I'm just about to find out." He pulled out his own headset. "I gotta see what's going on in there."

"Really?" I asked. "All this nature and you want to go back to school?"

Noah looked at his headset and then at the cabin window. He nodded. "Sure. Why not?"

"I thought we could get a test in before lunch," I said. "Not with the chemicals. Just a flight test."

Noah sighed and shoved his headset back into his bag. "You're probably right. That guy's survival bunker rattled me a bit too."

"Yeah," I agreed. "Maybe Sam and Amy's project will beat his if ours doesn't. I'd like *anyone* to win besides him."

After we put our stuff away, I grabbed two rockets, some engines, and our launch pad. Then we headed down a trail toward the large clearing Noah had spotted on the map. It wasn't long before we stepped out of the woods and into a glade about ninety meters in diameter. We marched to the center of the open space and set up a launch pad.

The pad consisted of a large metal base with two thin metal rods jutting up. It had placements for ten more rods, which we would use when we eventually launched all twelve rockets. As for now, we threaded two rockets onto the rods using the small sections of plastic straw glued to their sides.

Noah attached the wires to the igniters poking out of the engines at the bottom of the rockets. Meanwhile, I unspooled the other ends of those wires to a safe distance.

"All clear," he said as he stepped back from the rockets.

When he was a safe distance away, I attached the other ends to my battery-powered trigger. "Going hot," I said.

The rocket engine is like a bottle rocket without a fuse. Instead of a fuse, a tiny igniter is placed inside, which looks like two wires connected by a match head.

When electricity from the trigger flows through those wires, the match head ignites and sets off the engine.

"All set?" I asked Noah.

"Let's light these candles," he replied.

I held my thumb over the button. "Counting down. Three . . . two . . . one . . . liftoff!"

I pressed the button and sparks shot out of the bottom of each rocket. In unison, they blasted off the launchpad and into the sky.

WHOOSH!

Now, in theory, they would shoot straight up. The first stage would ignite the second stage and they would continue to fly completely vertical. There was no wind, so this is what was *supposed* to happen.

Guess what? That didn't happen.

Instead, when the second stage ignited, the rockets veered away from each other. By the time their parachutes deployed, they were high above the woods on either side of the clearing. Luckily, the booster stages fell into the clearing itself.

"What happened?" I asked. "Were their fins out of alignment?"

Noah shook his head. "No way. I checked and

rechecked those," he said. "That's what took me so long to assemble them. Besides, I can see one of them going out of alignment, but two at once?"

I watched the parachutes slowly drift down toward the trees. "If we lose them, we'll never know for sure."

"On it," Noah announced as he ran toward the tree line.

I took off toward the opposite side. I craned my neck to keep an eye on the plummeting parachute and the neon green (thanks, Dad!) rocket section.

As I entered the trees, I had to keep glancing down so I wouldn't trip over a log or run into a tree. Unfortunately, after looking away for the fifth time, I lost sight of the rocket. I jogged through the forest, heading for where I saw it last.

I ran onto a trail and looked around at the ground. The forest canopy had some openings, so there was a good chance the rocket made it to the forest floor without being snagged on a branch. But I didn't spot it anywhere.

Giving up on the ground, I scanned the branches above. It didn't take long for me to spot the neon green standing out from the leaves. Of course that color was easy to spot, because it was right next to a large patch of bright blue. I moved closer and saw a boy sitting high up in a tree. He held the rocket in his outstretched hand.

"Looking for this?" asked the boy. He sat on a thick branch and wore a bright blue shirt. He was from Liniford.

I was almost speechless with surprise. "Uh . . . uh . . . yes, thanks," I finally replied.

"Okay, here it comes," said the boy. He let it fall from his hand and the parachute inflated once more. I ran under the rocket as it floated toward the ground and landed in my outstretched hand.

"Thanks," I said. "What are you doing up there?"

"Installing my invention," the boy replied. He pointed to the base of his tree. "Look down there."

I stepped closer and saw a small, rustic birdhouse strapped to the side of the tree. But instead of having the usual hole for birds to enter, there were two USB ports under a placard that read TREE OF CHARGE. I visually traced the wires leading up from the top of the house and saw them spread out to springs and cables. They stretched to a few surrounding trees and were painted brown so you really had to concentrate to spot them.

"When the wind moves the trees, it charges my battery," the boy explained. "And it stores enough power to charge a phone or a tablet."

"Very cool idea," I said.

"Thanks," the boy replied.

I held up the rocket. "And thanks for this. I'm Tom, by the way."

"I'm Jason," he said. "And it wasn't a problem. It landed in a branch really close to me."

I gave him a wave and headed back the way I had come. I couldn't wait to tell Noah about Jason's invention. It was an ingenious idea.

It turned my thoughts back to our failed test as I walked. What could have made it go so wrong? Why did they fly so far off course?

I absently ran a finger over one of the rocket fins, and my fingertip caught on something. I stopped and examined the fin closely. There was a four-centimeter slice down one of the fins. If it didn't look so clean, I would have chalked it up to being damaged when it fell through the treetops. No, this cut was deliberate.

Someone had sabotaged our rocket.

8

The Incapacitation Complication

"YEAH," NOAH SAID. "SAME THING. RIGHT HERE!"
He pointed to the rocket he had recovered. It had the same tiny cut down one of the tailfins.

"No wonder they went haywire," I said. "As soon as the wind caught that cut, it created enough drag to pull it to one side."

"And the drag threw it off course," Noah finished. "Do you think all of our rockets have cuts like these?"

I shrugged. "What are the chances that we chose the only two out of all twelve that were damaged?"

"Let's get back and check," Noah replied.

We gathered up the rocket pieces and launch equipment before heading back to the cabin. We didn't speak the entire way, keeping a fast pace that would've made it difficult to talk anyway. If Noah felt the same way I did, then we were both too anxious about the other rockets to slow down.

I was racking my brain trying to figure out when someone could have sabotaged our rockets. Before we came to camp, the bin had been with us the entire time. And when it wasn't with us, it was locked inside the panel truck. Of course, it was out of our sight when it was delivered to our cabin by the camp counselors. I couldn't see why they would want to vandalize our project. And how would they have the time? If all twelve rockets were damaged in the same way, then that would have taken meticulous work.

That left Terry and Toby, our cabinmates. Sure, they were both plugged into their VR headsets when we arrived, but what if that was just an act? After all, the vandalism of the other projects happened while we were still at school. That ruled out both the students from the other schools and the camp counselors. If Terry and Toby were the vandals, they could have watched us approach and put on the headsets to throw us off. But still, it didn't seem like enough time to damage all twelve rockets, even for them. After all, Noah and I didn't spend *that* much time in Andrew's cabin.

I shook my head. I would have loved, loved, *loved* to make Andrew Foger the prime suspect. It totally sounds like something he would do. But unfortunately, he had the perfect alibi—me!

We made it to the cabin and raced inside. There was no sign of Toby, but Terry still sat in his bed, wearing his headset. Noah and I walked past him and knelt on either side of the container, carefully examining the rest of our rockets. Sure enough, every single one of them had a tiny slit down one of the fins.

"I don't believe it," Noah said. "What are we going to do now? There's no way these will fly straight."

"We repair them," I replied. "That's what we do."

"How?" asked Noah. "We can't replace the fins and have time for them to dry."

"We could create identical slits on all the fins," I suggested. "Balance them out."

Noah shook his head. "I don't think we could match them well enough."

We were in a bind. To repair the rockets correctly, we would have to replace all the fins. But that would take almost as long as building the rockets from scratch. There had to be a simple solution to made these rockets fly straight.

I snapped my fingers. Sometimes the simplest solutions were the best. "What about tape?"

"Tape?" asked Noah. "Are you kidding me?"

"Hear me out," I said. "We cut three identical pieces of tape, so the weight won't be off. We cover the slit with one piece and add tape to the other fins to balance everything out."

Noah opened his mouth to protest but then stopped. "That might work," he finally said.

"Long enough for us to seed one big cloud," I added.

"I like it," Noah said. Then his smile disappeared. "Now, the big question is, who did this?"

We both turned and stared at Terry. Unless he was really good at faking it, he didn't even know we were in the cabin.

Noah and I walked over to Terry's bed. I tapped him on the shoulder. Terry pressed a button on his controller and then raised his VR goggles.

"Hey, guys," he said. "What's up?"

I pointed to our open bin. "Did you see anyone in here earlier, messing with our stuff?"

Terry shook his head. "No, but I've been checking out Noah's program since I got here." He offered a fist to Noah. "Great job, man. But you should see some of the mods in there now."

Noah gave him a fist bump. "Yeah, I haven't had time to yet." He jutted a thumb over his shoulder. "So it's just been you and Toby in here the entire time?"

Terry nodded. "Yeah, I'm pretty sure." He leaned over to look past us. "Something happen to your project?"

"I think so," I replied. "Is yours okay?"

Terry removed his headset and hopped off the bed. "It better be." He picked up what looked like a plastic suitcase and set it on his bed. "Yeah, I heard that Samantha Watson was messing with people's inventions back at school," Terry said. "But no girls allowed in boys' cabins, right?"

I felt a rock form in my stomach. "No, that's not true," I told him. "That's just a rumor."

"Oh, okay," said Terry. He popped open the case to reveal what looked like a remote-control boat cradled in solid foam.

Terry and Toby had created a cool hydrofoil to test on the lake. In theory, it would race smoothly along the surface of the water no matter how choppy it got.

Terry pulled the boat out of the foam and turned it over in his hands. "This looks okay to me," he said. Then he examined the bottom. "Hey, the seam's coming apart here."

Noah and I leaned in to get a better look. Sure enough, the seam at the bottom of the boat was coming apart. There was a small mar near the center as if someone had pried it open with a knife or small screwdriver.

"Oh man," Terry said shaking his head. "We have to fix this. Otherwise this thing will fill with water and end up at the bottom of the lake." He grabbed his VR headset and pulled out his phone. "I have to get Toby back here." He stood and moved his phone around the cabin. "Aw, man. Can't get a signal."

"How were you accessing the virtual academy?" I asked.

"Through the Internet," Terry replied. "The Wi-Fi is great out here. The cell service, not so much."

"Where is Toby?" I asked.

"He went to lunch," Terry replied. "Are you guys

going? Can you tell him what happened?"

"Sure," said Noah.

"So, you don't think Samantha did this?" Terry asked. He pointed to the marred part of the boat. "It's obvious someone did something."

I shook my head. "I know it wasn't her. The rumor got started because I was joking about her messing with people's projects."

"Really?" Terry squinted up at me. "I thought you two were friends."

I imagined Sam's special death glare when she found out about the rumor. A shiver ran down my back. *I hope we are still friends*, I thought.

Noah and I left the cabin and hiked down the main road toward the chow hall. It was great being tucked away and having the most privacy, but our group of cabins were literally the farthest from the front of the camp. That meant that if you wanted to get to a meal on time, you had to think ahead.

We passed Andrew Foger's survival cabin. The two main doors were closed over the inner door. Looked like we didn't have to deal with Andrew again, for the time being.

We passed the odd student here and there but most everyone must have been at lunch. However, as we came around the last bend and the chow hall came into view, two familiar figures marched up the road toward us.

"Swift," Sam said as they moved closer. She wore the beginnings of the glare.

I immediately lost my appetite.

I raised my hands. "I'm sorry. I tried to stop it," I explained.

"He did." Noah pointed at me. "He really did."

Sam's eyes narrowed. "Tried to stop what, exactly?"

"The rumor," I replied.

Sam gasped. "What? You knew about this and didn't tell me?"

"Well . . . yeah . . . I guess," I shrugged. "Look, I was trying to stop it before you heard about it."

Sam's brow furrowed as she shook her head. "Why wouldn't you just tell me?"

I sighed. "Because . . . because it was all my fault." I glanced at Noah and Amy. "I'm the one who was joking about you being the vandal."

Sam ran a hand through her short brown hair and just stared at me. It wasn't the death glare; it was much worse. She stared at me with a look of utter disappointment.

Finally, she threw up her hands. "Well, guess what, Swift? From what we've heard, almost everyone's projects have been vandalized."

Amy nodded. "It's true."

"How?" I asked.

Sam shrugged. "I don't know. But now people think I messed with everything before we left the school."

Amy shook her head. "And she didn't."

"Of course she didn't," I said.

Sam's eyes widened. "Well, *I* know I didn't. But does anyone believe me?"

Noah cringed. "I'm guessing no?"

"That's right," Sam said. "And do you know why they don't believe me?"

I opened my mouth to take a guess but Amy beat me to it. "Because our project wasn't vandalized," she answered.

"And because of that, I just spent the last half hour being grilled by Mr. Edge," Sam added.

Noah and I glanced at each other.

"Oh man," Noah said. "Whoever did it must've heard about the rumor."

Sam nodded. "And purposely skipped us to make me look guilty."

"Did Mr. Edge believe you?" asked Noah.

"I think so," she replied. "At least he said he did."

"I'm so sorry, Sam," I said. "This is all my fault."

Sam shook her head and looked at me in disbelief. "You just don't get it, do you?"

My answering stare must have confirmed this, because she rolled her eyes and stormed down the main road, toward the girls' cabins. Amy gave a quick shrug and followed her.

The Observation
Objective

NOAH AND I WENT TO THE MESS HALL AND EACH grabbed a tray of lunch. I'd never been to summer camp before, so I didn't know what to expect when it came to the quality of the food. Unfortunately, I couldn't really say if the food was good or not because I don't think anything would've tasted good at that point. It was as if I couldn't taste anything with Sam being upset with me.

And I wasn't the only one who was upset. The long table where the Swift Academy students sat seemed somewhat subdued. The two other long tables on either side were occupied by kids from Bradley and

Liniford, and they chatted excitedly with each other as they ate.

"Don't worry," Mr. Edge told my fellow classmates. "I've talked to Mr. Alexander and he's helping with our investigation. We'll not only figure out who did this, but you'll also each have time to make repairs to your projects."

The Swift students grumbled in response.

"We already *know* who did it," said one of the grumblers. I didn't see who it was.

Mr. Edge raised his hands. "The other teachers and I take this sort of thing very seriously," he said. "But we can't make snap decisions based on rumors."

The kids weren't buying it. They shook their heads and glared even more than before. They seemed to be one step away from getting torches and pitchforks. Someone had to do something. And, unfortunately, I felt myself getting to my feet. I guess that someone was me.

"Uh . . . can I have your attention, please?" I asked, addressing the group.

My fellow students quieted and gazed in my direction. Kids from the other schools also took interest.

I nervously rubbed the back of my neck. "I just wanted to debunk this rumor about Sam vandalizing everyone's projects." Now that I had all the Swift students' undivided attention, my stomach churned and my palms began to sweat. I rubbed them against my jeans as I continued. "I know Sam is my friend and all, but I can say for a fact that the rumor isn't true."

"How do you know?" asked Kevin Ryan.

I cringed. "Because I accidentally started the rumor when I was just joking around."

The students began talking among themselves. I couldn't make out what everyone was saying, but it seemed as if some were buying my story, while others were not.

Kevin raised his hand. "Was *your* project sabotaged?" he asked.

I was about to say, *Yes, yes it was.*

But suddenly I found the seed of a plan to help clear Sam's name. It wasn't all there yet, but for it to work, I had to be evasive with my answer.

"We're all good," I said. It wasn't *quite* a lie. I just hoped Noah kept a good poker face, because my plan had just begun to sprout its first leaf.

Kevin nodded. "Right, because Sam's your friend. She wouldn't mess up your project."

Many of the students rumbled in agreement.

"That's not true," I said. "I mean . . . she wouldn't mess up *anyone's* project."

And . . . I lost their attention. My fellow students began several breakout discussions. Some seemed to believe me. Others speculated whether Sam would or would not vandalize a friend's project to make herself look innocent.

Mr. Edge stood and tried to defuse the situation. "Or maybe nobody's to blame," he suggested. "What I've seen so far could've just as easily been cases of something being damaged during transport." He shrugged. "Next year we'll make sure everything is packed more securely."

Noah and I exchanged a look. We knew that the damage to our rockets was intentional. A cut on a fin or two, maybe. But for all of them to have deliberate damage was way more than coincidental. Then there was Terry and Toby's boat. It couldn't have been packed more safely if they had tried.

That reminded me. I slid out of the table and quickly

located Toby Nguyen. "Terry said that there was some damage to your boat," I told him.

"Aw, man," Toby said as he rose from the table. He dumped his tray and disappeared out the main door. I went back to my seat beside Noah.

"What was all that 'we're good' stuff you told Kevin?" he asked. "You know someone messed with our rockets."

"Yeah, but what if the vandal thought that we hadn't noticed anything?" I asked. "And nobody knows we had a test launch today."

"So?" Noah shook his head. "Why do you care if anyone else knows?"

I grinned and lowered my voice. "I'm thinking we can set a trap for whoever did this."

"What are you talking about, Tom?" he asked with a grimace. "Who are we, Scooby and Shaggy?"

I laughed. "Not that kind of trap." I glanced around to make sure no one was listening. "I'm just talking about a way to flush them out. Find out who it is."

Noah rolled his eyes. "Man, I just want to fix our rockets and finish our project."

"Don't you want to prove Sam didn't vandalize anything?" I asked.

"Of course I do," Noah replied. "I just don't see how we can do that."

"What if we could do both?" I asked him.

Noah smirked. "All right, big-idea man. How are we going to do that?"

I pulled out my phone and checked my weather app. "Good," I said. "It's supposed to be cloudy tomorrow morning. The humidity looks good too. Hopefully the clouds will be low enough."

"So we launch tomorrow?" asked Noah.

"Right," I replied. Then I raised a finger. "Hold that thought." I stood and addressed the Swift Academy students once more. "Uh, can I have your attention once again?" I asked. I waited for the conversations to die down before continuing. "Just so you know, if you're going to be at the north end of the camp tomorrow, you'd better have an umbrella." I gave a wide grin. "Noah and I are going to launch our cloud-seeding rockets at around . . ." I glanced down at Noah. "Eight o'clock?" I asked him. He just shrugged. "Eight o'clock," I repeated more confidently.

I sat back down and various discussions continued.

"What was that all about?" Noah asked.

"Simple. We get to conduct our experiment," I replied. "*And* anyone who shows an interest gets put on the short list of vandal suspects."

"Why would he or she want to see our experiment?" asked Noah.

I smiled. "Since we supposedly don't know anything is wrong with our rockets, they're due to fly off in twelve different directions tomorrow. Who wouldn't want to see that?"

Noah matched my smile. "I know I would."

We finished our lunch and went back to our cabin. We were going to need as much time as possible to repair our rockets. On the way back, we crossed paths with Jenna, hiking and charging. I told her about our upcoming test. If anyone can spread news, it's her.

Noah and I spent the rest of the day working on the rockets. Now, putting tape on each fin doesn't sound like a big deal. But when each piece of tape has to be measured out precisely and placed in exactly the same spot on every fin, it takes a lot longer than you would think. It was painstaking work. I calculated that the added weight of the tape would cost us a couple of meters in altitude. Amy would've been able to give me precise calculations, but she wasn't returning my e-mails.

By the time we were finished, we decided not to leave our rockets unattended until the launch. So for dinner, Noah went to the chow hall and brought food back for us.

Later that night, Mr. Alexander scheduled some kind of campfire presentation for everyone. It sounded like a good distraction, so I went and Noah stayed behind—he wanted to stay and watch over our rockets. There were songs, skits by the camp counselors—it was kind of cool, actually. But fun aside, I mainly went hoping to run into Sam or Amy—except neither of them was there. In fact, there was a low Swift Academy turnout in general.

I'm guessing Noah and I weren't the only ones trying to salvage our sabotaged project.

And that brought up another question. Why just the Swift Academy experiments? Did someone have a beef with the entire school? I thought maybe one of the camp counselors might've done it, since they had access to all the gear. Then I thought it might be someone from another school. But in either case, why just target

Swift Academy? Oddly enough, it made the most sense that it was someone from our school, since the sabotage began before we even got to camp.

By the time I made it back to our cabin, I was exhausted and ready to turn in early. But when I found Noah sitting on the edge of his bed wearing his VR headset, I was wide-awake and irritated.

"Dude," I said. "You're supposed to be guarding our stuff."

Noah pushed the visor up onto his forehead. "I have the volume off," he explained. "No one's been in here since you left. I guarantee it."

"You guarantee it, huh?" I asked.

"Yup," he replied.

I guess I believed him. But don't get me wrong. I still opened our bin and looked over our rockets, just to be sure.

"Man, wait until you see what people did with my program," Noah said. "On the second floor . . ."

"Dude, spoilers," I said, cutting him off.

"You're right," he said. "I don't want to ruin the surprise." He pointed to his headset. "You want to check it out?"

I shook my head. "Some other time. I'm going to look up the weather again, and recheck our calculations."

I did just that while Noah returned to his virtual Swift Academy. Soon after, we turned in for the night.

After a not-so-restful night's sleep (Terry Stephenson snores like an idling motorcycle), it was my turn to run out and get breakfast. Again, I didn't see Sam or Amy there. I couldn't tell if I just missed them or if they were avoiding everyone because of the rumor.

When I returned, Noah and I gathered our equipment and we ate on the run. We had to make it to the field and get set up by eight o'clock. Not only was that when I had told the entire camp that we were doing our experiment, but it also happened to be the best time of the day for weather conditions. The clouds were low in the sky and the humidity was high. That means there were some fat clouds just hanging there, waiting for our rockets to push that humidity over the edge and into rain territory.

When we arrived at the field, we got to work. Our new setup was slightly more complicated than the one for our previous test. We were launching twelve rockets, so they had to be attached to twelve metal guide rods. Twelve rockets also meant twelve igniters and twelve wires leading to the trigger. Of course, to complicate matters, we planned to launch the rockets in four salvos—three rockets at a time. Luckily, we had loaded all the chemicals into each rocket's payload area the night before. This was all about launch arrangement and management.

While Noah finished wiring up the rockets, I moved to the edge of the clearing and attached my phone to a tripod. Since the schools' attending teachers and competition judges couldn't be all over the camp at once, we had to record our experiment and findings to show them later. I got a nice angle of the rockets with plenty of room to catch them in flight. Noah was going handheld, making sure he caught anything my phone missed.

"What's the time?" I asked Noah.

He checked his phone. "Seven fifty-five."

I scanned the woods around the clearing. There was no one else around. Here we were, almost ready to launch, and no one had bothered to show up.

So much for my big plan. I sighed. Maybe I *would've* done better concocting some kind of Scooby-Doo trap.

Noah glanced around and shrugged. "No one came," he said.

"Yeah, I know," I admitted. "Let's just concentrate on the experiment."

"Sounds good to me," Noah said. He pressed a button on his phone and turned it around. "Newton and Swift cloud-seeding project." He aimed the phone back at the rockets and took a step back.

"Going hot," I announced as I flipped the main power switch. "Launching in three, two, one . . ." I pressed the first launch button.

WHOOSH!

Three rockets shot off the launchpad. I pressed the second launch button.

WHOOSH!

Three more rockets took off. I pressed the third launch button.

WHOOSH!

The last three rockets raced toward the sky. Every one of them shot straight up; not one of them flew off course.

Noah aimed his phone at the rockets as they soared high above us. Almost in perfect unison, the first three rockets ignited their second stages. Their three booster stages fell toward the ground as the rockets soared higher and higher until they disappeared into the low clouds. The rest of the rockets did the same until they all vanished. Now there was nothing to do but wait.

Then I saw something out of the corner of my eye—a flash of bright green. I turned and spotted someone at the far edge of the clearing. It looked as if someone came to watch us after all—someone wearing a Bradley shirt.

From this distance, I couldn't make out who the person was. And as I squinted my eyes and stared a bit longer, the person darted away, running deeper into the woods.

"Hey!" I shouted as I took off after them.

"Tom?" Noah asked.

"I see our guy!" I exclaimed, and ran toward the edge of the clearing. Soon Noah was right behind me.

When we hit the woods, we darted around trees and ducked under low branches. Just like when I was chasing the rocket, we kept having to look down to avoid tripping. But this time, our target was a green shirt that was getting smaller and smaller. The spy was getting away.

And after ten more meters, I found out why. We ran out of the woods and onto an open trail. That was why the person was making better time. He or she didn't have to dodge trees and fallen branches. We took advantage of the open space ourselves and hastened into a sprint.

We had lost sight of the green shirt around a corner but caught a glimpse of it again during a long straightaway.

"There he is," I said. "Come on!"

Our footfalls echoed down the trail as we poured on even more speed. When we lost sight of it again around a winding turn, we moved even faster. Hopefully, we could close enough distance to at least identify the suspect.

Unfortunately, that wasn't going to happen.

"Whoa," Noah said as we turned onto another straightaway.

We both slowed considerably as we entered a large fog bank. It began as a few tendrils snaking across the trail. But the farther we traveled, the thicker the fog became. We eventually had to stop completely so we wouldn't run smack into a tree.

"It's no good . . . we lost him," Noah said, panting heavily. "Let's go . . . get our gear."

"I'll meet you . . . back there," I said, breathing hard myself. "I'm not . . . giving up yet."

Noah nodded and backed out the way we had come. I found myself alone in a disorienting field of white. I carefully inched forward.

The strange fog came on so quickly and was so localized that I knew it couldn't be a natural occurrence.

"Mia?" I shouted. "You got some more fog fluid, I see."

"Who's that?" came Mia's disembodied voice. She sounded close.

"It's Tom," I replied. "Where are you?"

There was no reply. Then a hand fell onto my shoulder and I jumped. Mia laughed as I spun around. She was still hard to see through the thick fog even though she was standing right beside me.

"Did you see someone run through here?" I asked.

Mia raised an eyebrow. "Are you kidding?"

Mia's project was similar to Evan's. But instead of harvesting water from moisture in the air, she created a special net that absorbed water from fog. Now, since she couldn't rely on a natural fog occurring, Mia had planned to borrow some of her father's special-effects fog machines and make her own fog. Instead of measuring the amount of water it absorbed, she would measure the amount of fog fluid.

I glanced around, trying to get my bearings. "All right, well, I'm passing through, so where's your net?"

Mia pointed past me. "It's strung up along the side of the trail, on the right. If you stay on the trail, you won't hit it."

"Thanks," I said as I began to shuffle forward. I kept my eyes on the ground so I could slowly move forward while staying on the trail.

I kept shuffling down the trail and I thought I spotted part of Mia's net strung across some trees on my right. It was too bad that her net wasn't strung across the trail itself. That way she could've caught the spy for me. As it was now, I just hoped that the fog slowed down the spy's progress enough so they didn't get too far ahead.

As the fog thinned, I picked up the pace. The more of my surroundings I could see, the faster I moved. Soon I was back to a full run, racing down the trail, until I came to a screeching halt.

The trail split off into two different directions. I had lost the spy.

10

The Corrugated Concealment

I WENT FROM ONE TRAIL TO ANOTHER, LOOKING for any kind of sign as to which one the spy had run down. But who was I kidding? I couldn't track someone through the woods like that. And even if I could, these were well-worn hiking trails in a summer camp. There was no way I could figure out which trail the spy had taken.

Darn it! I spun on my heels, heading back toward the clearing. So much for my big plan.

"Hey, Tom," greeted a voice.

I stopped and spun back around. There was no one

on either trail in front of me. I peered into the woods beside me. I was alone.

"Up here," said the voice.

I looked up and spotted Jason high in one of the pine trees. Once again, he straddled a branch and had wires and cables running past him. I followed them down to spot another little Tree of Charge birdhouse attached to the lower trunk of the tree.

"Jason," I said. "How many of those are you putting in?"

He shrugged. "Ten in all," he replied. "I'm calculating their efficiency based on topography, weather patterns, forest density . . ."

"That's really interesting," I interrupted. "And I'd love to hear all about it. Really. But right now, can you tell me if you saw someone run through here a second ago? Someone in a green shirt?"

"Oh, yeah," Jason said. He pointed to the trail on the left. "He just ran down this trail."

"Thanks," I said as I started down the trail.

"But he didn't stay on the trail," Jason continued.

I skidded to a stop. "Where did he go?"

"He cut into the woods on the left," Jason explained.

My shoulders drooped. How was I supposed to follow his trail through the woods?

"And then," Jason continued, "he came out near the main road and headed toward that big shipping container. I think he went inside. It's hard to make out from here."

"Shipping container?" I asked. For a second there, I had no idea what he was talking about.

"Yeah, you know," Jason replied. "That rich kid's survival cabin. He's been showing it off to anyone who will listen."

A grin spread across my face. "Thanks!" I shouted as I took off down the trail. I cut left, into the forest, ducked a few more branches, and then burst through to the main road. It was right next to—you guessed it—Andrew Foger's cabin.

There were two windows I could peek through to find out who had been spying on us. Unfortunately, there were the occasional student and teacher walking up the main road. The last thing I needed was *Peeping Tom* as a new nickname.

Instead of going to the windows, I tried to casually stroll toward the main doorway, as if I visit all the time.

The outer doors were open but the inner door was shut. Once I was inside the small entrance area, I was out of view from the road. Then I could peer through the small window in the door.

Keeping low, I crept up to the door and eased toward the window. Standing just inside were the usual suspects from before: Andrew, Mike, and Mark. However, Mike (or maybe Mark) was bent over, trying to catch his breath.

"Well?" asked Andrew. "Don't keep us in suspense. But if you're going to hurl, do it outside."

The out-of-breath twin gave a dismissive wave. Then he stood straighter. "Their rockets were fine," he reported between breaths. "They went off without a hitch."

"What?!" Andrew asked. "I was assured those rockets would be out of control, flying all over the place." He shook his head. "What's the point of having someone on the inside if they're not going to do their job?"

I caught my breath. Andrew had someone on the inside? Inside Swift Academy? Could he really do that? Have one of our own students work against us?

"And why are you huffing and puffing, anyway?" Andrew asked.

"Tom spotted me and chased me," the twin replied.

The three of them turned their heads toward the door, and I ducked. I closed my eyes and held my breath.

"Did he follow you back here?" asked Andrew. I heard footsteps growing louder.

"Naw, I lost him," Mike or Mark replied.

I didn't have enough time to run out of the entryway. Instead, I made the bonehead move of crouching down and picking up one of the large empty boxes beside the door. I pulled it over my body and plopped to the floor, sitting cross-legged.

Noah and I used to play a video game where the main character would sometimes hide under a box the same way. We made fun of it because it seemed so ridiculous. If you're guarding a high-security military complex, then of course there's nothing suspicious about a cardboard box sitting in the middle of a hallway.

I was already kicking myself. My subconscious must've remembered that game—why else would I choose such a dumb hiding spot? Let me put it this way: My supersecret camouflage was so bad that when Andrew opened the door, he actually kicked the side of the box with his foot.

"I thought you were going to get rid of these," he told one of the twins.

I grimaced as the box began to rise off the floor.

"Not now, you moron," Andrew said. "I want to go see what Swift is up to. Show me where they are."

The box dropped back to the ground and I was in darkness once more. Three sets of footsteps moved away from me.

I couldn't believe that actually worked. Wait until I told Noah. . . .

CLANK! CLANK!

I heard the main doors slam shut. You remember those, right? They're the doors that can only be opened from the outside.

The Artificial Expedition

I THREW THE BOX OFF AND RAN TOWARD THE doors. I almost pounded on them. But just before my fist hit metal, I paused. What if I slid through one of the windows instead? I could sneak out that way and nobody would know that I had been there in the first place.

I went back to the inner door and turned the knob, sighing with relief when it opened. I felt a little guilty as I stepped inside the cabin. But then again, Andrew did invite us to stop by anytime.

I sprinted to one of the windows and peeked out. A

couple of students walked past on the nearby road, but I didn't see Andrew or the twins. They must've already walked down the trail, into the woods. I was in the clear.

I reached up, preparing to open the window, and a rock formed in my stomach. The window was solid; it wasn't meant to open. I checked the other one. It didn't open either. I glanced around the cabin and goose bumps formed on my skin. There was no way out.

I needed another plan. I was pretty sure that Andrew didn't lock the outer doors. Theoretically, anyone could open them from the outside. I just needed to get someone's attention.

I reached up and knocked on the window, trying to get someone to notice me. Unfortunately, the windows were built with two pieces of clear plastic. The panes were layered several centimeters apart from each other, so I'm sure they were very well insulated against hot or cold temperatures. Of course, this also made them insulated against sound, too. As much as I knocked on the inner plastic pane, no passersby seemed to notice. I finally gave up after the tenth person passed without hearing me.

"Okay," I said out loud. "Time for Plan C." I would

just have to call Noah and have him come and free me. I reached for my phone and moaned with disappointment. Why, you ask? My phone was back at the clearing, attached to a tripod. Okay, I really needed a Plan D.

I sighed and plopped down on the couch. There was nothing to do but wait for Andrew to return and deal with the consequences.

I looked at the big-screen television and considered watching a movie or playing a video game. But I didn't think I could relax enough to do either, even if it was just to pass the time.

I sat in silence for a few minutes until I heard faint voices. Were Andrew and the twins headed back already? I turned toward the door but no one entered. Then I heard the voices again, still just as faint.

I glanced down and noticed a VR headset on the couch beside me. Of course it was one of those expensive high-end jobs, with a built-in microphone and headphones. With sound still coming from the headphones, it looked as if someone was in the middle of a game and left the device on.

I picked up the visor and put it on. What kind of VR game were Andrew and his goons playing?

I inhaled sharply when I saw the outside of the Swift Academy there in the viewscreen. How did Andrew Foger get access to Noah's game? The only people who knew about it were academy students. Then again, the virtual school wasn't exactly a big secret. If Andrew had someone vandalizing Swift Academy inventions, why wouldn't he or she share the login information for Noah's game?

I adjusted the headset's speakers and microphone. Then I picked up the left- and righthand controllers. If I was going to be stuck there in the cabin, I might as well pass the time checking out some of the new mods in Noah's program.

As I stood there on the front steps of the virtual school, two more avatars appeared out of thin air.

"He's supposed to meet us in the gym," one said to the other before they both ran up the stairs and through the main entrance.

That's why I heard voices before I put on the headset! While Noah made it so only the four of us spawned in the basement, everyone else began the program outside the school.

I moved my avatar up the steps and through the main door. Inside, everything looked fairly normal.

Well, normal for a video-game version of our school.

"Dum-dum-dum!" came a voice from the administration office. I moved into the offices and down the back hall. I turned into the principal's office and burst into laughter. Mr. Davenport stood on top of his desk wearing nothing but tighty-whities and a flowing red cape. Some Swift Academy student had actually dressed our principal as Captain Underpants.

I backed out of the office and hoped that I wouldn't crack up the next time I ran into Mr. Davenport in real life.

I moved my avatar into the main hallway and toward the gym. I saw a few other avatars come and go, and the sounds of cheers grew as I moved farther down the hall. When I got to the gym entrance and peeked inside, I was amazed at what I saw. Our school gymnasium was now the size of a large coliseum. The stands were full, and the audience roared with delight as several monster trucks raced, jumped, and crushed one another in the dirt field below.

Now, there weren't enough Swift Academy students to fill a quarter of that coliseum so I guessed that the audience members weren't avatars of real people. But I would bet that the monster truck drivers were all students. Anyone can go see a monster truck show, but how else would a kid get to drive one?

I considered making my way down and hopping into one of the monster trucks. But then a thought occurred to me. What if I told one of the avatars that I was trapped in the cabin? It would almost be as good as flagging someone down from the window.

Except most of the avatars in the virtual school probably didn't represent students actually at the summer camp. Sure, I had seen a few people at camp with VR headsets, but that was a small percentage of the amount of avatars I had already seen in the game. And I hadn't even made it off the first floor yet. Plus, with all the Swift students at camp repairing their vandalized projects, I doubted any of them had time to stroll the virtual halls like I was.

I supposed I could tell one of the students to text Noah and tell him to let me out of the cabin. And even if Noah was somewhere in the camp with decent cell service, that still left another problem: I didn't know who the vandal was. It could be any avatar I ran into.

That only left one option. All I had to do was get to the basement and leave a message for Noah, Sam, or

Amy. Sure, Sam and Amy didn't know about the cabin, but Noah did.

I backed out of the gym and headed for the stairs. Unfortunately, with the gym now a huge monster-truck-battle dome, I got turned around and headed to the east stairwell by mistake. Just like in the real school, only the west stairwell went down to the basement.

I spun around and went back the way I had come. As I neared the gym, a huge monster truck tire flew through the open doorway.

CRASH!

The tire smashed into the wall just a few feet in front of me. The entire hallway was now blocked by a giant tire and twisted school lockers. I couldn't get to the basement from there.

Noah had mentioned that the game would reset at some point, but I didn't know how long that would take. Instead of waiting, I turned around and headed back for the east stairwell. I would simply go up to the second floor, cut across, and get to the west stairwell on that side.

I hit the stairs and ran up to the next level. When I reached the second floor, I saw that someone had spray-painted a red *Z* over the number 2 in FLOOR 2. I didn't know what that meant, but I spotted the virtual spray paint can on the floor. I made my avatar pick up the can and activate the button. Red paint squirted from the nozzle. Perfect. Now I could leave a message for my friends.

As I walked out onto the second floor, the creep factor dialed up to eleven. The entire floor was deserted and looked like it had been decorated for the apocalypse. Shredded books and splintered desks littered the area. Fluorescent lights flickered and a smoky haze filled the air. My avatar was the only one there.

Whoever made this mod to the program did an excellent job. I actually felt my heart beat faster just by being immersed in such an eerie environment.

I slowly inched forward. I thought about zipping down the dark corridor as fast as I could, but something gave me pause. Maybe it was the creepy scenery, or the instincts I had picked up from every horror movie I'd ever seen. But it was a good thing I didn't run blindly down the corridor.

Shambling figures began to exit every doorway on the floor. Just one or two shuffled from the classrooms closest to me. But steady streams poured out of the doorways at the far end of the corridor, and the entire second floor slowly filled with zombies.

These zombies looked very realistic—too realistic. My heart beat faster as I began to back out, returning the way I had come, but at that point I had already passed a couple of classrooms. Four zombies were behind me, blocking my escape.

Even though it was against my instincts, I thought about letting one of the zombies kill me. That way, I would respawn back in front of the school and I could just skip this floor altogether. But I didn't know how many lives my character had or if this game even worked that way. With everyone going in and making changes to the program, there was no telling what would happen if my avatar was killed.

"Look out," a voice said as a large figure pushed me aside.

A woman in glinting silver armor drew a long broadsword and attacked the nearest zombie. It disappeared when her blade slashed through it. She made quick work of the other three before guiding me back to the stairwell.

"Who runs the zombie gauntlet with just a can of

spray paint?" the woman asked. At least, she sounded like a woman. There were the electronic hints of a voice modulator at work there.

I held up the can, forgetting I was holding it. "First time here?" I replied.

The stairwell was better lit and I could make out more of my rescuer. She was a good foot and a half taller than me, had curly black hair, and wore a gleaming helmet that matched her suit of armor. The helmet had white wings on either side. She was a formidable figure from Norse mythology—a Valkyrie.

"I'm trying to get to the . . ." I almost said "basement." Only the four of us knew the code to get into the basement. Noah would kill me if he found out I let other people know about our secret room. They'd be bugging him for days trying to get the code out of him. "I'm trying to get to the first floor," I told her.

The Valkyrie pointed down the stairs.

"On the other side," I specified. "The monster truck tire blocked it off."

"Ah," said the woman. "Happens all the time." She turned and moved up the stairs. "We'll have to cross the third floor. I hope no one's triggered the dinosaurs yet."

"Dinosaurs?" I asked as I followed her up the stairs. "As in, plural? I thought there was just the one T. rex."

The Valkyrie stopped and turned to me. "And I thought this was your first time here."

"I heard about it," I said.

I waited for her to continue up the stairs, but she didn't. Instead, her avatar just stared at me.

"Who are you, by the way?" I asked.

"Anonymous," she replied, before continuing up the stairs.

"What a coincidence," I said as I followed. "Me too."

I was thinking about asking the Valkyrie avatar for help with my little entrapment problem. But when she acted so suspiciously, I thought it best to stick with my original plan. After all, if this were the vandal, or a friend of the vandal, then I would be playing right into his or her hands.

We entered the third-floor landing and ran down the long corridor. "Looks like we got lucky," the Valkyrie said.

Everything was quiet until we passed the biology classroom. Two other avatars ran out of the room just before the giant T. rex crashed through the wall.

"Not so lucky," I said as we ran toward the other stairwell.

As we neared our goal, the Valkyrie drew her sword. "Keep running," she ordered. "I'll hold them off. I've fought them before."

I didn't have to be told twice. I kept my avatar moving as two classroom doors burst open behind me. I glanced back to see a Velociraptor leap out of each doorway. The Valkyrie batted one away with her sword but the other one leaped onto her back. It clawed at her armor while the other dinosaur recovered and moved in. All the while, the T. rex thundered down the hallway behind them.

I didn't feel great about it, but I ran down the stairwell as fast my avatar could move. The Valkyrie had a sword and a suit of armor. All I had was a lousy can of spray paint. There was nothing I could do to help and I knew it.

I made it down all three flights of stairs and into the basement level. It really looked just like the real one. Just beyond the stairs, a security door blocked access to the basement floor. I ran up to the door and raised a hand toward the keypad. I carefully had my avatar enter eight, three, eight, four—just like the real access code in our school. The door opened and I stepped inside.

This part of the school looked just as it was when Noah first showed us the game. Even though he turned it over to the other students to change, they couldn't get to this part of the virtual school, both in the game and in the code. Only the four of us had access.

I raised the virtual spray can and began to leave my message on the wall. It took a while and I had to write in giant letters so the spray-paint lines would be legible, but I got it done. When I was finished, my message covered a huge portion of the basement wall.

Trapped in Andrew Foger's cabin.
Please help. ~Tom

Now there was just one more thing to do. I had to take this avatar and leave it somewhere outside the basement. I stepped out of the basement door and found myself face-to-face with the Valkyrie.

"How did you get in there?" asked the Valkyrie.

"Uh—" I stammered. I didn't know what to say. It turns out I didn't have to say anything.

Suddenly, the VR visor was pulled off my head! And just like that, I was ripped out of the virtual world. I left the basement and the Valkyrie behind to find myself back in the real world. Back in Andrew's cabin. Except I wasn't alone anymore.

"How did you get in here?!" Andrew Foger asked.

The Delusion
Conclusion

I DON'T KNOW IF IT WAS BEING RIPPED OUT OF the virtual world or the fact that I was startled by the arrival of Andrew and the twins. Maybe it was a little of both. Either way, a chill rippled through my body and I was in full-on fight-or-flight mode. My eyes darted toward the door.

Mark and Mike must've caught my look. They split up and moved around the couch, flanking me.

I shrugged. "You said to drop by anytime," I said, trying to lighten the mood.

Andrew stabbed at my chest with the VR visor. "This

is trespassing, Swift. Breaking and entering. You're gonna get into so much trouble for this."

I flicked his hand away. "What about vandalizing inventions?" I asked. "Think you might get into a little trouble for that?"

Andrew exchanged a quick glance with the twins. "What is that supposed to mean?" he asked.

I nodded. "I heard you talking all about it."

"Oh yeah? Prove it." Andrew grinned and crossed his arms. "I haven't touched anyone's anything."

"No, you got someone from our school to do it," I said. "Who was it? Who did you talk into doing your dirty work for you?"

"That's for me to know . . . ," Andrew began.

"And for you to find out," I finished for him. "Yeah, yeah, I remember. Well, wait until *everyone* finds out what you did." I tried to step around the couch to leave, but one of the twins shoved me back.

"Hey, it's your word against mine," Andrew said.

My eyes narrowed. "I can be very convincing."

Andrew threw up his hands. "Okay. You got me. I wanted Bradley to get the grant this year. And since your dad is too good to work for my dad, I wanted every invention in your stupid school to fail." He turned and jutted a thumb at the door. "I'll even go to the teachers right now and confess everything."

"Oh really?" I asked skeptically. I narrowed my eyes. "That seems quite reasonable of you." Too reasonable.

"Oh, sure," he replied. "And I'll tell them how your friend Samantha was the one who helped me. Simple as that."

"That's not true," I said.

"Yeah, but they don't know that," Andrew said. "Everyone already thinks she's guilty, right?"

There was that stupid rumor again.

"So, you can keep your mouth shut," Andrew said. "Or I can take your friend down with me. What'll it be?"

I felt another rock in the pit of my stomach. Not only did I start the stupid rumor, but now this guy was going to implicate her if I said something.

The only thing that made me feel better was imagining what Sam would do in a situation like this. Sure, she didn't like being wrongfully accused of something. Who would? But I know my friend; I know there is no way she would let a bully like Andrew win, no matter what the risk. She would definitely call his bluff.

"I say we help him make up his mind," said Mark or Mike. They both took a step forward, closing in on me.

"What's it going to be, Swift?" Andrew asked. "All or nothing."

I shrugged. "Nothing, I guess."

I snatched the VR visor from his hands and tossed it into the air. When Andrew leaned forward to catch it, I climbed over the couch and jumped off the back. I darted through the door and out of the cabin before the three of them could touch me.

I chanced a glance back as I ran down the main road. The three of them rushed out of the cabin and sprinted after me. I turned and ran as fast as I could.

The rest of the road was deserted. Everyone must have been either busy with their own experiments or on their way to lunch.

I thought about running all the way to the chow hall, but that was a long distance to keep up such a fast pace. I decided to try to lose them down one of the hiking trails. I turned right into the first trailhead I spotted, and darted down the twisting trail.

If I had the map with me, had time to memorize it, or if I knew the camp better, I'm sure I could've quickly taken trails all the way back to the clearing where we had launched our rockets. And I'm sure Noah would be furious when I saw him—he had to pick up all the rocket components by himself. But I had no doubt he'd cut me a break when he found out what I knew *and* saw who was chasing me.

Now, however, I just concentrated on losing Andrew and the twins. I zipped down every side trail I came across, trying to throw them off.

I turned a corner and spotted a fallen tree a couple of yards off the trail. I hopped off the path and ran for it as fast as I could. The trunk wasn't as wide as I would've liked, but I hoped it would be big enough to hide my bright yellow Swift Academy T-shirt. I jumped over the tree and threw myself to the ground. I listened carefully for footsteps.

It wasn't long before I heard the three of them run past. Their footsteps faded, and I counted off fifteen seconds before I slowly peeked out from behind the tree.

I was completely alone. Carefully and quietly, I made my way back to the trail. Once safely on the well-worn path, I ran back the way I had come. Hopefully, I had bought myself enough time to find help.

It was hard to believe that Andrew had arranged to have everyone's projects vandalized simply to win the grant. Maybe his father wasn't as well off as Andrew had made him out to be. Or, more than likely, Andrew was simply targeting the Swift Academy because of my father and me. He certainly was the type to hold a grudge. But what was really unbelievable was the fact he could talk someone in the academy into doing his dirty work. I didn't want to believe Andrew, but how else could the projects have been vandalized *before* we arrived at camp?

I put that out of my head and concentrated on the path, trying to retrace my exact route. I slowed when I reached a split in the trail. Coming from the other direction, I couldn't tell from which side I had come. I came to a complete stop, concentrating on every tree, every log, looking for something familiar.

My gut tightened. I was wasting too much time. They could double back at any second.

Then I saw something on the left trail that made my decision for me. I took that trail and ran. Up ahead, through the trees, I saw a swatch of bright yellow floating through the forest. Another Swift Academy student was on the path ahead of me.

I closed the distance between us as fast as I could. I rounded another corner and spotted the student at the end of a long straightaway.

"Hey!" I shouted.

The student turned. It was Jenna Davis, hiking as always.

Jenna stopped to let me catch up. I was out of breath by the time I got to her, and she waited patiently while I bent over and panted.

"Can I borrow . . . your phone real quick?" I asked between breaths.

"Sure," Jenna said. She dug into her pocket and pulled out her cell. "I don't know if you'll get a signal, though. The best places that I've found are in the main parking lot and near the boathouse."

"Wow, you have been all over this place," I said as I took her phone and examined the signal strength. No bars. I handed the phone back to her.

"Excellent Wi-Fi, though," she said.

"Can you e-mail Noah for me?" I asked.

"Sure," Jenna replied. She pulled up her mail program.

I gave her Noah's e-mail address and then began my message. "Tell him to find Mr. Edge or Mr. Alexander."

She typed while I bent over again to catch my breath. "Tell him that Andrew is the one behind the vandalism. And he has an accomplice. Someone from our school is helping him."

Immediately, it felt like I breathed a little easier, both from catching my breath and finally getting a message out about Andrew.

But then Jenna stopped typing. She simply stared at me with wide eyes, terrified.

Had Andrew caught up with me? I glanced over my shoulder, but there was nothing there. I turned back to Jenna, and that's when it hit me.

"Oh man," I muttered. "You're the accomplice."

13

The Surreptitious Surveillance

"I'M SORRY, I'M SORRY," JENNA SAID, TEARS welling in her eyes.

I shook my head in disbelief. "Why?" I asked.

Jenna wrung her hands and stared at the ground. "My stepbrother goes to Bradley. When Andrew found out that Patrick had a stepsister at the Swift, he made Patrick's life miserable. This was the only way I could get him to leave my brother alone."

"Didn't your stepbrother just report him?" I asked.

Jenna nodded. "It didn't matter. Because of his father,

Andrew's basically untouchable if there isn't any physical evidence against him."

So that was why Andrew was so confident about his word against mine. Andrew didn't sabotage anything himself, he had someone to do it for him—his very own virtual vandal. So there was no physical evidence against Andrew in this case, either.

"I tried to only do little things," Jenna explained. "Things that could be easily repaired. I hid in the back of the panel truck and messed with everyone's projects on the way to the camp."

My lips tightened. "Except for Sam and Amy's project."

Jenna nodded. "I didn't mean to start that rumor, really. But once Andrew found out about it, he spread it some more. And he told me not to damage her invention."

"He said if he went down, he was bringing Sam with him," I told her. "You can't let that happen. You have to tell people what really happened."

Jenna closed her eyes and shook her head. "I can't. I'm sorry, but I have to help my brother."

"Look, I'll back you up," I said. "My dad has some pull too, you know."

I never liked using my name or my father for any special treatment. For Sam's sake, however, I would make an exception. After all, it seemed as if Andrew didn't have any reservations about using his father to get what he wanted.

Jenna wiped her eyes. "Do you think it'll actually . . ." Then she looked over my shoulder and gasped.

I spun around and saw three green shirts growing larger through the foliage. Three Bradley students were coming up the trail, and I had a feeling who those students were.

"Come on," I said, grabbing her hand. I got Jenna moving as we ran up the trail away from the approaching bullies.

"Can you get us back to the main road?" I asked.

"This way," she said as she pulled forward, taking the lead. Her hiking boots must have been charging on overdrive while we ran up the winding trail.

The trail dumped out onto the main road very close to Andrew's cabin. I stopped and bent over again, panting. After all that, I'd ended up right back where I started.

I glanced around and, just as before, the main road

was deserted. We couldn't find anyone to help and we couldn't keep running.

"Quick, send that e-mail to Noah," I told her.

"Okay," Jenna said. She pulled out her phone and began tapping at the screen.

"Tell him to get to Andrew's cabin quick," I added.

I glanced back and saw Andrew and the twins getting closer. I just hoped that Jenna would send the e-mail out before Andrew got there and talked her out of it. I knew firsthand just how intimidating he could be.

"Done," Jenna said.

"Is this quick enough for you?" asked a familiar voice.

I gasped in surprise as Noah, Sam, and Amy exited Andrew's cabin.

"How did you get here so quickly?" I asked.

"We got your note," Sam replied. "Well, Amy got your note."

I laughed with surprise. I had completely forgotten about my spray-painted message in the virtual basement.

"You've been playing the game, Amy?" I asked.

"We both have," Sam said. "Once our digger gets going, it's pretty low-maintenance."

"When did you find my message?" I asked.

"I was there when you wrote it," Amy replied.

"Really?" I asked. Then I turned to Noah. "You gave her the invisibility hack and not me?"

"I wasn't invisible," Amy said. "I was right there."

"Wait, you weren't . . ." I knew exactly who she was. "You were the Valkyrie."

Amy nodded. "And when your avatar stopped moving, I figured you had left the game. But I could still hear everything through your headset microphone."

I grinned. "You heard all that?"

"Not only that . . ." She tapped a button on her phone and Andrew's voice emitted from the speaker. "'I wanted Bradley to get the grant this year. And since your dad is too good to work for my dad, I wanted every invention in your stupid school to fail.'"

"Hey," said Andrew's voice. Everyone turned to see him and the twins strolling across the road, all out of breath.

"Don't worry," Amy said. "I e-mailed an audio file to Mr. Edge and Mr. Alexander."

"Nice touch, Ames," Noah said, giving her a fist bump.

"How?" Andrew asked between breaths. "How did she get that?"

"Well," I said with a wide grin, "that's for me to know and you to find out."

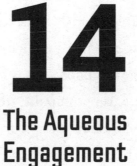

The Aqueous
Engagement

"INCOMING!" I SHOUTED.

Noah glanced around. "Where?"

Before I could reply, a blue water balloon smashed into Noah's chest. It exploded on impact, drenching his entire upper body.

Noah gave out a loud gasp. "That's freezing! Are they chilling those things?!"

"Oh man. I think so," I replied.

When Liniford had set up across the field, I noticed that they carried their water balloons in ice chests.

I thought they just used the chests to store them, but clearly they had employed extreme tactics.

The large field was divided into three sections, with each school controlling a third. Like us, many of the students seemed to put just as much thought into their water-balloon siege weapons as they did their conservation projects. There were catapults, trebuchets, and even a huge slingshot-crossbow design from Liniford—the very same one that had just drenched Noah.

Noah shivered. "Lame, lame, lame!"

Of course, that wasn't the first time Noah was wet that weekend. As far as our experiment went, it was a good news-bad news sort of thing. The bad news was we were unable to replicate our findings because all of our rockets were warped during the first test. The good news was that *rain* and cardboard rockets don't mix.

That's right. If I hadn't kept going after Mark (or was it Mike?) then I would've seen the complete success of our cloud-seeding project! The rockets ejected their payloads into the targeted cloud and a positive reaction was attained. In other words, we created a very localized rainstorm—eight milliliters' worth! With the data we collected, we theorized ways to scale up the rockets for bigger and better results that would still remain portable.

FOOMP!

Sam fired one of our launchers at the group of Bradley students. "Now?" she asked as she reloaded.

I looked down at Amy. She sat on the ground and worked under the large tarp covering our secret weapon. "Not yet," Amy said from beneath the tarp.

Even though Andrew and the twins weren't among the Bradley students, Sam seemed to target them the most. It turned out that Amy's audio evidence was enough to get Andrew and his lackeys sent home. A large truck pulling a flatbed trailer drove in and hauled away Andrew's cabin soon after. I didn't know if the three of them were going to be expelled from Bradley or not. I guessed Andrew would find out just how much pull his father really has.

FOOMP!

I fired a balloon at a group of Liniford students. It soared toward them, but they easily sidestepped it.

For her part, Jenna Davis was sent home too. I had no idea how Mr. Davenport would punish her for sabotaging everyone's projects. Hopefully he'd take into account that the damage was minimal, as well as the extenuating circumstances involving her brother.

"Look out!" Sam shouted. She darted out of the way just as Bradley's slingshot fired another round.

Noah was busy lining up a shot at Liniford, so he didn't see the incoming balloon.

SPLAT!

"Yee-ow!" It hit him in the back of the thigh.

Sam grinned at me, trying to hold in a laugh.

I was glad Sam wasn't angry with me anymore. It turns out that she wasn't mad at me for starting the rumor. She was angry that I didn't immediately tell her when I first heard about it. That's what she was talking about that day. I really should've just told her right away, instead of trying to stop it behind her back.

FOOMP!

I lobbed another round toward Bradley. I didn't even keep watching to see if it hit anyone. After all, it was mainly a distraction, anyway. I reloaded and checked on Amy again.

"What do you think?" I asked her.

"Almost there," she replied, looking down the field and then back under the tarp. I could see her mind racing through the calculations. She was in her element.

Amy and Sam's project ended up coming in third place. Their well digger had only dug down six feet, but it proved to be an inexpensive and effective way to dig wells for those in need of clean drinking water.

A Bradley invention, the Litterbot 3000, came in second place. It was pretty much an automated outdoor vacuum cleaner. With all the leaves and twigs on the ground, I never would have thought something like that was possible. But it had a ninety-to-ten ratio of litter to natural debris.

But the coolest surprise was first place going to Jason's Tree of Charge. All ten of his installations had been a success. They worked so well that Mr. Alexander even compensated him so the charging stations could stay up throughout the next summer camp season.

FOOMP!

Noah launched another round at Liniford. "Anytime, Ames," he said.

"You know I don't work well under pressure," she said as she dug under the tarp.

Luckily, she looked up just in time to see another incoming round. She squeaked and flattened to the ground as the speeding water balloon zipped over her head and—you guessed it—hit Noah instead.

"Oh, come on!" he shouted. "Freezing!"

The main flaw with most everyone's water balloon machines was the speed. The catapults, trebuchets, and even our pneumatic launchers—they all *lobbed* water balloons. By the time the balloon made it to the other side of the field, people could easily dodge the slow-moving round.

Liniford's slingshot, on the other hand, did *not* lob. It shot balloons straight across the field, making them extremely difficult to dodge. Add that to the fact that the Liniford students chilled their water balloons, and they quickly became everyone's prime target.

"Okay, all set," Amy announced. She stood and unwound the long remote cord. Then she pulled off the tarp to reveal our secret weapon.

Just like our rockets, we had twelve launchers mounted to a sheet of plywood. It looked intimidating with twelve PVC pipes aimed almost straight up. Each pipe was loaded with yellow water balloons, nestled in our specially designed shuttles. The entire thing was powered by a large air tank, also hidden under the tarp until ready.

"Oh yeah," said Sam.

"Let's do this," Noah added.

"Fire when ready," I ordered.

"Okay," Amy said as she pressed the firing button.

F-F-Foo-Foo-F-Foo-Foom! Foo-F-F-Foo-Foo-Foom!

The sound was so strange that everyone on the battle-field paused to see what had just gone off. The next moment couldn't have been more perfect. The entire Liniford slingshot crew was center stage when they were suddenly pummeled by twelve water balloons from above. Sam, Noah, and I lobbed three more over to them while they were distracted.

All the Swift and Bradley students cheered as Liniford got drenched.

"Nice shooting, Amy!" Sam said.

"Perfect!" Noah added.

Amy smiled at me. "What do you say, Tom?"

"I say . . ." I grinned at my team. "Reload!"

DON'T MISS TOM'S NEXT ADVENTURE!
- The Spybot Invasion -

The Recovery
Discovery

"ARE YOU SURE YOU'RE NOT GOING TO BE SICK?"
Ms. Ramos asked. She held out a kidney-shaped plastic basin.

I waved it away with the fingers on my right hand. "No, I'm okay." Even though I still felt a little queasy, the container looked way too small to do any good if I got sick.

I sat hunched over on the edge of the exam table in the nurse's office. My entire airbag suit was still inflated, so I was more propped on the edge than sitting.

Ms. Ramos eyed me suspiciously as she pulled out

a pair of medical shears. "You still look a little green." She took the shears and carefully cut the clear plastic airbag helmet surrounding most of my head. Air hissed out as she moved on to my right arm. Once she pulled the deflated plastic away from my body, she produced an instant cold pack. She squeezed the pack and gave it a shake before placing it into my free hand. "Hold this to your forehead," she said. "It'll help."

As I placed the cool pack against my skin, Ms. Ramos put the shears to work again. She carefully deflated more airbag sections, and I let out a deep breath. The ice pack did work; I felt less nauseated.

"What were you thinking, Tom?" Ms. Ramos asked. "You could've seriously hurt yourself."

"We already tested it on a dummy," I explained. "It was time to test it on a real person."

Ms. Ramos shook her head. "Do you remember when I went to every class and showed you how to perform CPR?"

"Yeah?" I said. I didn't know where she was going with this.

She continued to deflate more airbags. "Well, I didn't demonstrate CPR on real people, did I?"

"No," I replied. "You used that dummy."

"Exactly," she said. "You don't test things like this on real people. I've actually performed CPR on a real person once, and even though it saved his life, it hurt him, too."

"You've done CPR for real?" I asked. "When was that?"

Ms. Ramos continued to free me from my inflated airbags. "When I was the nurse at my last school, a man came to speak to the students. Unfortunately, his heart stopped and I had to perform CPR on him until the ambulance arrived."

"Wow," I said. "So, you saved his life?"

Ms. Ramos shook her head. "Yes, but that's not the point." She aimed the shears at me. "After everything he went through, the bruising from my chest compressions took the longest to heal."

"Yeah, but still," I said. "You saved his life. That must've felt pretty good."

Ms. Ramos smiled. "At the time it was terrifying. But now, yeah, it does feel good."

I couldn't even imagine doing something as big as saving someone's life. Sure, Ms. Ramos had always done a great job taking care of us. Just last month she had performed the Heimlich maneuver on Charlie Wells when he was choking in the school cafeteria. But I can imagine that in a school like the academy, you'd never know what kind of injury a school nurse could run across. With everyone working on so many different inventions, experiments, and unusual school projects, Ms. Ramos might be treating small burns one day and minor frostbite the next. It felt . . . nice, having someone like her around.

"I want to save someone's life," I said, almost without thinking.

Ms. Ramos raised an eyebrow and paused her airbag-suit removal.

"I—I mean," I stammered. "I think it would be cool to come up with an invention that could save someone's life."

She deflated the last part of my airbag suit. "Well, you're off to a good start," she said, then pointed to my arm. "These sections on your arms and legs are already similar to inflatable splints."

"That's a thing already?" I asked.

"Sure," she replied. "For when someone breaks an arm or a leg. You blow the splint up and they keep the limb immobile so you can move the patient."

"Oh," I said. "I guess I'll have to come up with something else."

She aimed her finger at me. "Promise me that you won't go testing your inventions on yourself again."

I nodded. "I promise."

I held up my arm and looked at the tattered remains of my airbag suit. It seemed kind of pathetic now, but I wondered if this could be my lifesaving invention. How cool would that be? Maybe it would save someone in a motorcycle crash. Or maybe an experimental test pilot could use it.

But this thing had a long way to go. I tugged at one of the clear strips hanging from my wrist. *It's back to the drawing board*, as my dad would say. Not only did this thing not deflate when it was supposed to, but there are tons of different scenarios that I'd have to account for to trigger such a device. I'd have to think of some other way to come up with a lifesaving invention. My mind raced with concepts and ideas.

Ms. Ramos put away the shears and reached out for my chin. She gently held it, turning my head slightly. "Your color is almost back to normal. How do you feel?"

"Just a little queasy," I said. I began to stand. "I'll be fine."

The nurse placed a firm hand on my shoulder. "I think you should wait here just a bit longer. Want me to call your father?"

My eyes widened. "No!" What was she doing? I thought she wanted my nausea to pass, not make it worse. "I mean, he'll find out about everything soon enough. No sense in ruining his day."

And my day, too, I thought.

She smiled and tousled my hair. "Okay, why don't you relax and lie back for a few minutes to let your stomach settle?"

I did as she instructed and closed my eyes. The cold pack felt soothing and the nausea continued to fade into nothingness. I heard Ms. Ramos milling around in her office before she left the room, and I lay alone in silence.

I tried to think of other inventions that could possibly save lives. I dove headfirst into the middle of one of my favorite parts of inventing—brainstorming. Here there were no wrong answers, no stupid ideas, and no limits. Could I invent a lifesaving drug? That would require years of medical school, but it was a possibility. Or I could always go the engineering route. Maybe I could create some sort of new surgical tool.

I opened my eyes and gazed about her office. Two framed photographs sat on her nearby desk. One showed a young boy and a girl—maybe eight or nine years old. The other photo showed a grinning little girl that was almost a toddler, and I felt myself smiling back at her as she proudly stood at what might be one of the first times. These must've been Ms. Ramos's kids. I wondered if they realized just how cool their mom really was.

My smile faded when I spotted an odd plastic figurine next to the photos. It had a squat, cartoonish body and an oversize head, with two batlike ears pointing straight up. Its two devilish eyes seemed to stare back at me. But what was most unsettling was its devious expression, with its mouth in the shape of a circle as if it were saying, *Oooooh*.

A small shiver went through my body. I reached over and spun the creepy figurine around so it faced the wall.

The Reiteration
Equation

MS. RAMOS CUT ME LOOSE IN TIME TO MAKE THE
second half of my physics class. I was no longer nauseated, but I decided to skip the stairs for the time being.
I headed to the elevator instead. I stepped inside and
pressed the button for the third floor.

"Hold the door, please," came a voice from the corridor.

It was Tristan Caudle. I held back the doors as he
glided into the elevator in his wheelchair. Jake Mahaley
jogged in behind him. I expected to get some ribbing
from my tumble down the stairs, but we rode the elevator up in silence.

"I didn't say anything," Jacob said suddenly. "I swear."

"Well then how else did he find out?" Tristan snapped back.

I nervously took half a step back from the bickering students. "Uh . . . is everything all right?" I asked.

"Everything's just great," Tristan said, rounding on me. "If getting a day's detention for calling Mr. Edge a moron is all right."

I cringed. "Whoa! To his face?"

Tristan shook his head. "No, I said if he thinks one day was enough to finish our assignment, then Mr. Edge is a moron." He jutted a thumb toward Jacob. "I told *him* that." He glared at his friend. "And *somehow* Mr. Edge found out about the moron part."

"Maybe someone else heard you say it," Jacob said. "You know I wouldn't do that to you."

The elevator door opened for the second floor and Tristan wheeled himself out. "Whatever," he mumbled.

Jacob ran out after him and the doors closed behind them. I was once again alone in the elevator.

Okay, that was weird, I thought. Just a little academy drama to make my elevator ride a bit more interesting, I guess.

I got out on the third floor and padded down the empty corridor. When I reached physics, I gently turned the handle and eased the door open. I was hoping to sneak into class without anyone making a big deal about my tumble. Luckily, all was quiet as Mrs. Lee scribbled out some formulas and figures on the digital board at the front of the classroom. She was notorious for calling out tardy students. She would often put them on the spot in a physics sort of way, asking things like how long it should've taken to get to class, calculating the distance from the restroom against the average speed of someone not wanting to be late, taking into account what kind of shoes they were wearing and things like that.

Fortunately, she continued to scribble on the board and I slinked in. The bun on the top of her head bounced up and down as she excitedly completed the work. So far, neither she nor anybody else saw me enter the classroom. If I was lucky, I'd be able to make it to my desk without anyone noticing.

I wasn't so lucky.